I0625892

Heidi Garrett

Beautiful Beautiful

A CONTEMPORY FAIRY TALE

Beautiful Beautiful by Heidi Garrett
Half-Faerie Publishing

Copyright © 2013 by Heidi Garrett

Find out more about Heidi Garrett at
www.heidigwrites.blogspot.com

All rights reserved.

This book is a work of fiction. Names, characters, places, brands,
media and incidents are either the product of the author's
imagination or are used fictitiously. Any resemblance to actual
persons, living or dead, actual events or locales is purely
coincidental.

All rights reserved. No part of this book may be used or reproduced
in any manner whatsoever without written permission except in the
case of brief quotations embodied in critical articles and reviews.
Thank you for respecting the hard work of the author.

Cover Art by J.W.B.
Design Concept by J. Gordon Smith

Editing by Vince Dickinson and Ken Wallin

ISBN: 978-0-9882068-5-4

Other Books by Heidi Garrett

Sign up for Heidi's newsletter!
http://eepurl.com/wWKUj

Daughter of Light

(A Young Adult Fantasy Trilogy)

Isolt's Enchantment, A Prequel
Half Faerie, #1
Half Mortal, #2
War & Grace, #3

Once Upon a Time Today

(A Collection of Stand-Alone Modern Fairy Tale Retellings)

The Girl Who Believed in Fairy Tales: Three Short Stories
Dreaming of the Sea
The Tree Hugger
I Am Lily Dane

In Collaboration with Billie Limpin

(A New Adult Paranormal Romance)

Cupcakes and Kisses

To my readers

Contents

Chapter 1: The Most Beautiful Boy in the World

Mirabella rolled off her father's back.

She giggled and snorted as she caught herself with her hands and launched onto her short, slender legs.

Her daddy reared up on his knees, twisted, and waved his arms over his head. "GRROWR!"

Seven-year-old Mibi dashed into the kitchen, screaming, "You can't catch me, Daddy!"

Her daddy collapsed on the floor. "Not even gonna try."

Kerrin slid from the sofa to cross her husband's body with hers. Lying stomach to stomach, she propped herself on her elbows, hands splayed over her eyes, acting as the lookout for their daughter's return.

When Mibi peeked out from the kitchen, Kerrin closed the space between her fingers. "I can't see you!"

Bare feet slapped the hardwood floor. When they became a muffled shuffle, Kerrin braced herself. Mibi threw her body against her parents—an exuberant torpedo of arms, legs, and laughter. Her daughter's thick, waist-length hair spilled over Kerrin's face as their three bodies collapsed into a flattened mass.

Mibi's arms clutched her mother's neck in a stranglehold. "Tell me the *beauty beauty* story."

"Are you sure that's the one you want tonight?"

Mibi let go of her mother's neck and patted her cheeks. "Yes!"

Almost every night Kerrin told her daughter a fairy tale. The bonding ritual had begun a few years ago on a trip. They'd forgotten to pack Mirabella's favorite bedtime stories, and Kerrin had improvised with a fairy tale, drawing symbolism from her personal history. The experiment had been such a success, they'd repeated it over and over.

Kerrin had discovered a creative way to pass meaningful lessons from her life on to her daughter, and Mibi cherished the opportunity to reshape the tale each time it was told by asking questions and interjecting her own opinions and commentary.

As Kerrin struggled to get up, her daughter cleaved to her side—an extension of her mother's body. Her husband offered them a hand. When they were steady on their feet, he brushed his wife's cheek with his lips and ran his hand over his daughter's hair.

That simple gesture reminded Kerrin why *beauty beauty* had become one of her favorite fairy tales to tell, in spite of its inherent challenges.

Kerrin transferred Mibi to her husband. When their daughter was secure in his arms, with her head nestled against his neck, they walked down the hall to Mibi's bedroom.

Daddy tucked Mibi in, and then turned off the overhead light and waved goodnight.

Kerrin flicked on the small lamp on the nightstand and

settled on the bed next to her daughter.

Mibi took hold of her mother's hand.

§ § §

"Once upon a time there was a girl who believed in beauty," Kerrin began, "and there wasn't an aspect of beauty that she couldn't appreciate."

"Did she have a Daddy?" Mibi asked.

"No, but she had a fairy godmother."

"What was the fairy godmother's name?"

"Hannah."

"What about her mother?"

"The girl's mother was possessed by a dark enchantment."

"What was her name?"

"Emery."

Mibi giggled. "That's Gramma's name."

"Yes, it is."

"Why did the girl like beauty so much?"

"Because she realized it was everywhere, and no matter how many things she lost, or how many things were taken away from her, or even how many things she'd never had in the first place, beauty was always available."

"Like a purple flower that grows in a broken sidewalk," Mibi said.

"A black panther stalking through the jungle." Kerrin imagined zooming in on the big cat with a lens.

"The snow before it gets dirty and melts."

"A rainbow after the storm has passed."

"My ballet shoes."

"My daughter."

Mibi beamed.

Before the birth of her daughter, Kerrin had feared years spent behind a camera might have stunted any maternal instinct she possessed. If anything, her observant eye increased her ability to tune in to Mibi's spirited personality.

§§§

Kerrin Mayham avoided eye contact with the other guests as she studied the room. It was her nature to balance and weigh every element: color; furnishings; space. Since she could remember, she assessed each detail of any new physical environment. Her eye sought asymmetry and dissonance as much as order and balance, measuring light and angles to frame the perfect shot in her mind.

"Kerrin."

Being interrupted before she settled the shot made her

anxious. That single decision, highly personal, made her feel secure, no matter where she was or who she was with. It had since she'd started playing her private game, decades ago.

She forced herself to smile at the president of the Golden Pinnacle Guild and the party's host. "Frank."

"Are you enjoying yourself?" he asked.

"It's an honor to be here."

He stopped one of the waitresses roving by with platters of champagne flutes, and handed Kerrin a glass. "Marais-Leroux-Delair."

She took a sip. "It's wonderful."

"Only the best to celebrate the Golden Pinnacle nominees. Are you nervous about the awards show tomorrow night?"

"Of course."

"Don't be," Frank said.

"Are you privy to inside information?" Probably everyone in the room had or would ask him that question tonight. A giggle escaped her lips. It was an embarrassing, nervous sound. She raised her glass and drained the remains. Swilling expensive champagne lacked grace, but as one of the top five female directors on the indie film circuit, Kerrin had learned it was better to break rules with conviction. Determination set trends. She flagged down the next waitress herself and handed Frank a glass.

"I know *A Scorched Heart* is a masterpiece." He tilted his head. "It was your vision that made every frame of that film a work of art."

Was he telling her that she'd won? It was hard to say. Maybe he fawned over all the nominees. She raised her glass in a toast anyway. "Thank you."

He sidled up to her, glancing around the room—a king surveying his subjects. "Benji!" Frank waved over a thirty-something guy with black ear studs and gnarly eyebrows. "Have you met Kerrin Mayham?"

The younger man shook her hand.

"Benji reps James Fellowes. You know him? Young guy, light hair, dark eyes, straight eyebrows." Frank's eyes twinkled.

She wondered if he thought Benji's eyebrows were gnarly too, but she couldn't place James Fellowes. But then all the hot actors in Glitter City looked like gods descended.

"Another young Adonis?" Kerrin asked.

"Yeah, him," Benji said.

"The studio's optioned this script," Frank continued, speaking to both of them. "Demion Glass. It's about a guy possessed by demons."

Horror wasn't Kerrin's thing. "I haven't heard of it." Her mind roamed. She swiveled her head in both directions. How was it possible there wasn't a single waitress in sight?

"We're going to offer it to the winner," Frank said.

"Actor of the Year?" she asked.

"Nah," Frank said, "Director of the Year."

He was talking to her.

"Have you ever worked with a studio budget, Kerrin?"

"No, it's always been indie for me."

"You've never really made a movie until you've worked with the big boys," Benji said.

She would not knee him in the groin.

Frank crossed his arms. "I came up on the indie circuit. Shoestring budgets are the best way to learn the nuts and bolts."

Benji wiped visible sweat from his brow with a cocktail napkin.

Frank patted him on the back. He took Kerrin's arm and led her away. "There's a few more people I'd like you to meet tonight."

§ § §

"So finding beauty helped the girl?" Mibi asked.

"Yes, it did. Whenever she was lonely or disappointed, she would go in search of the most beautiful thing she could find that day. When she found it, her troubles slipped away."

"How did she know when she found it?"

"Her heart would feel like it could fly."

"I don't have any troubles."

Kerrin smiled at her daughter's failure to recall the minor complaints she'd voiced earlier that evening. "Someday you might. Everyone does."

However, gazing at her daughter, Kerrin intuitively understood the challenges in Mibi's life would be different than the ones she'd faced. She doubted there would be a Tom in her future. With Mibi's father so involved in his daughter's life, she wouldn't need a father figure. The thought lightened Kerrin's heart. Tom had been a desperate, reckless mistake. Although not her only one.

"I'm going to be the only person on the planet who doesn't have any troubles!" Mibi brought Kerrin back from her musings.

"But if you ever do—"

"Mommy, I'll remember to look for something beautiful."

§§§

Sherri Winestine, the aging, yet sleek agent for Bruce Rik, was the next person Frank introduced Kerrin to. He definitely had an agenda.

Her heart floated. Would the rest of the nominees receive similar treatment before the night was over or had Frank singled her out?

A frumpy woman approached with a young god in tow. Kerrin blinked. He really could be Adonis wearing a faded green t-shirt, worn chinos, and rubber flip-flops. Had to be an actor. The raw talent that generated every light in Glitter City, actors got away with everything. Inappropriate attire was the least of the social crimes they were forgiven.

Kerrin glanced up at the recessed light fixtures. A ricochet of shadow?

No, the closer he got the better he looked.

So scrubbed and fresh. The fingers of her right hand curled. God, she needed her camcorder.

"Frank!" the frumpy woman shouted.

The host held out both his arms. The woman almost bowled

him over with her enthusiasm for his embrace. He closed his eyes and patted her back.

The woman yanked on Adonis' hand as if he were her five-year-old son. "Here he is. The one I told you about. Anthony Zorr." She made an impressive maneuver, exiting the close embrace with Frank to shove her beautiful find in his face.

Sherri wandered off.

Anthony grinned.

Dawn shimmered across a rising tide.

Kerrin lost track of the conversation. All she saw were those cheekbones, those masculine bow lips, and that stance—not bloated and beefy, just taut. And tan. He glistened. Standing with his hands jammed into his pockets, he gave off an air of bashfulness.

Where had he come from?

She re-tuned to the conversation. Ah, just off the bus and all the way from the cornfields in Iowa. He wouldn't stay untouched for much longer. Kerrin wanted him—she didn't know for which film, and she didn't care. She just wanted him in front of her camera, filling frame after frame with that natural boyish exuberance at the edge of becoming a man.

"How old are you?" Kerrin asked.

Anthony, the woman with him, and Frank looked at her as if something living had gotten caught between her teeth.

"Ma'am?"

He had called her ma'am. She couldn't decide whether it was endearing or insulting. Maybe a little of both.

Kerrin pressed on. There were at least four other directors in this room who would lure him, hook him, steal him away from her. She wasn't going to let them. "My name is Kerrin Mayham."

He took her proffered hand. "Right on."

His handshake was firm, dry. The promise of that simple physical exchange charged her body.

"Kerrin Mayham!" the frumpy woman blared.

All the heads in the room turned in their direction. Kerrin flattened her hand against her thigh to resist the reflex to cover her ear.

Oblivious to the foghorn effect of her voice, the woman continued. "I'm such a fan of yours! I've seen every single film you've ever made. Anthony is twenty-four. He has a great look, don't you think?"

"Yes," Kerrin said.

"And he's not just a pretty face. He's won awards."

She assumed for acting. "That's great," Kerrin said.

"Anthony, Kerrin's one of the five directors nominated for the Director of the Year," Frank said.

"Nice to meet you, ma'am."

There it was again. That ma'am. "Please, call me Kerrin."

"Have you met Marni Lamb?" Frank asked. "She's an agent with Colossal Talent."

The frumpy woman wedged herself between Kerrin and Frank. "We've met now."

Kerrin was again impressed with the physical agility of someone so rectangular. Anthony spread his legs and settled his arms in reverse fig leaf. Kerrin imagined camera angles. Vivid expression. Anthony blessed her with another shy smile.

Marni squeezed Kerrin's arm with two hands. "Anthony's going to make a huge splash in Glitter City," she said. "First film—he'll be a star. I know these things."

Kerrin couldn't disagree.

"What do you think, Frank?" Marni pointed to her client. "Is he Demion Glass or what?"

Frank slid his index finger along his eyebrow. "It's possible. Absolutely, possible. Bring him by to meet Glenda next week."

"You want to wait that long? Another studio will snap him

up tomorrow." She actually chucked Anthony under the chin, and he allowed her to do so.

Midwest polite?

"It's going to be crazy the next few days," Frank said.

Marni waved her hand. "I know. I know. It always is when the Pinnacle winners are announced. But you don't want to let this one slip away, do you? Glenda could spare five minutes for me."

"Tell her I told you to squeeze him in as soon as possible. How's that?"

"Oh, that's perfect." Marni squeezed her hands into baby-like fists and bounced them up and down. "You won't regret it."

She gave Frank another bear hug and squeezed Kerrin with equal enthusiasm before dragging Anthony away.

"That's Marni," Frank said. "She'll hit all the studio heads tonight." He stopped one of the waitresses, took two glasses from her tray, and offered one to Kerrin.

She didn't want any more champagne.

Watching Anthony's back, all Kerrin yearned for was her camera.

§§§

14

"One day the girl met the most beautiful boy in the world," Kerrin said.

"Mommy, boys aren't beautiful."

She ruffled her daughter's hair. "You might change your mind about that one day."

Mibi stuck her index finger in her mouth and pretended to gag.

"If you'd seen this boy, you would have thought he was beautiful too."

"What color were his eyes?"

"The color of the ocean on a bright, clear day."

"What color was his hair?"

"Gold like a wheat field."

"Did the girl fall in love with the boy?"

No matter how many times Kerrin told her daughter *beauty beauty*, Mibi always asked *that* question. She returned her daughter's mischievous grin. Mibi was too young for an overt discussion on the ins and outs of animal magnetism. Kerrin just hoped the truth in her embellished tale would seep into her daughter's subconscious, a protective seed that would blossom if it was ever needed.

Chapter 2: Magic Shoes

The doorbell rang.

"Would you get that, Norah?"

Joanie worked on Kerrin's chignon. That morning, Norah and Joanie had taken Kerrin to breakfast. The three had spent the rest of the day at the spa together. Then her two friends had followed her home.

"You've got company," Norah yelled from the hall.

"I wasn't expecting anyone," Kerrin called back.

"You'll want to see these people. I'm bringing them into the bedroom."

"Is she kidding?" Joanie pulled her hands away from Kerrin's head.

Kerrin frowned as her hair fell from the loose knot that wasn't really working.

She glanced around her bedroom. It looked like a moving company had delivered a roomful of boxes and up-ended each one before they'd left. She'd been hunting for her grandmother's rhinestone pumps. The ones Hannah had worn on her wedding day, eighty years ago.

As far as Kerrin was concerned, they were magic shoes, and if she wore them, she'd definitely win. The problem was that she'd forgotten about them until two hours ago. They'd been shoved out of the way, along with a lot of other stuff Kerrin had never bothered to unpack when she'd moved into her home.

Now they perched on the rosewood chest at the end of her bed, like Dorothy's ruby slippers. But the rest of the room was a wreck.

Norah led a young man and woman through the pile of boxes. Dressed casually, the man in jeans, the woman in leggings, they tactfully ignored the mess.

Kerrin smiled at them before crossing her eyes at Norah. Joanie cleared off one of the chairs, trying to create a place for one of them to sit.

Norah handed Kerrin a creamy envelope and velvet embossed box. "Frank's studio sent these, along with Mel and Lynn to do your hair and makeup."

Kerrin's name was written on the envelope in calligraphy. Things like this didn't happen when you directed indie films. By the time shooting was over, you were fortunate if there was any budget left for a wrap party.

"If you'll sit down–" Lynn pointed to the vanity. "–I'll get started on your makeup. Mel will do you hair."

Norah raised her eyebrows as Kerrin ripped open the envelope. "Frank looks forward to seeing me tonight."

Joanie made a crude gesture.

Kerrin nodded her head toward Lynn and Mel, who were waiting patiently for her to sit, so they could do what they'd come to do.

"Open the damn box," Norah said.

Kerrin handed her Frank's note. Her hands shook as she opened the expensive case. When she saw what was inside–an exquisite diamond choker–she couldn't help but exclaim.

Joanie squealed and slapped her butt. The girl had a one-track mind.

"It's going to look perfect with your gown," Norah said.

The backdrop of the final, breath-stopping scene in *A Scorched Heart* was a setting sun. A nod to those closing frames, the colors in her sunset-inspired gown progressed from a blue-gray bandeau bodice, through lavender, gold, and orange, to end in a fierce train of red.

Her gaze roamed over the chaos of boxes. Bittersweet memory tugged Kerrin's heart. In one of them was a junkyard crown—one she'd used to play dress up when she was a child.

"Honey, that bling would make a dirty sheet look good." Joanie brought her back to the present.

Kerrin couldn't laugh at the lame joke. She was too touched by a sense of enchantment. "It was made to go with my grandmother's shoes."

§§§

Mibi clapped her hands. "Magic shoes!"

"Made of diamonds," Kerrin exaggerated.

"Were they expensive?"

"They were a gift from her fairy godmother."

Mibi folded her arms across her chest. "I wish I had a fairy godmother."

"I'm sorry, honey, only orphans get fairy godmothers."

"Was the girl an orphan?"

"Yes."

"That's sad," Mibi said.

"It is."

"So she got magic shoes instead of a family?"

"Something like that."

"What happened next?"

§§§

Sweat pooled in Kerrin's armpits, making her gown tacky. The ceremony had already lasted more than three hours. The entire audience in the Pavilion Theater wilted. Only four awards left. Next up: Best Director.

Kerrin forced herself to take a slow, deep breath.

The five-film montage began. The crowd searched for the five nominated directors as overhead cams swiveled. Sitting in the midst of the cast and crew of *A Scorching Heart* braced her. They'd be jubilant if she won.

She was going to win.

Kerrin forced herself to watch each video clip as it exploded across the enormous flat screen centered above the main stage.

Her heart beat a racy tattoo. She'd seen all these movies before —two of them she'd studied, but only now could she admit: The competition was fierce.

Applause erupted around her. The pivotal scene in *A Scorching Heart* played on the monitors. Even if she didn't take home the award tonight, it was clear to her, and judging by their response, the entire audience, that her indie step-child held its own against the four major studio projects.

No matter what happened, she could take pride in that.

Jenna Lee and Blake Jones crossed the stage.

People patted Kerrin's back, wishing her luck. Someone shouted, "Yeah, Kerrin!"

When Jenna ripped into the envelope, Kerrin stared at her left foot. The toe of her rhinestone pump winked with reflective light.

Her grandmother had been the one to notice Kerrin's eye for beauty, image, and detail. On her tenth birthday, it had been Hannah who'd given her granddaughter her first camera, an Eklin GN, and 10 rolls of 35mm black and white film. She still had it.

Emery, Kerrin's mother, had been furious with the

extravagant present, but Hannah had told her granddaughter not to worry. Emery only burned with envy because she'd never bothered to develop her own talents—squandering her life on drugs and bad men instead.

Blake's voice ripped Kerrin from the past, "And the winner of the Golden Pinnacle Best Director of the Year is—!"

"—Kerrin Mayham!" Jenna Lee beamed.

Music blared. A lightning bolt of joy ignited Kerrin's body. Everyone around her stood up. They grabbed her arms and hands. Exuberant congratulations fell like confetti. Somehow she made it to the aisle. So many people—some she recognized, some were strangers—all stood up as she walked by. They smiled and waved.

She ascended the steps.

One of the Golden Pinnacle girls pushed the elongated, gold pyramid into her hands. Kerrin wiped her eyes.

She advanced to the podium. Blake shook her hand. Jenna Lee hugged her and squealed in her ear.

In a surreal daze, Kerrin faced the audience. The people who believed she deserved this award.

She couldn't remember a time when she'd felt more alive.

§§§

23

"The girl had to compete in a contest," Kerrin said.

"What kind of a kind contest?" Mibi asked.

"It was a contest to see who could make the most beautiful thing."

"Did she win?"

"Not until she learned to believe in herself."

"How do you believe in yourself?"

"Whenever you decide to do something—or create something—that's going to require a lot of hard work, you trust yourself. And then do the best you can do. You don't give up."

Mibi shrugged. "Okay, but what about the boy?"

§§§

Kerrin had never kissed more cheeks or shaken more hands. She longed to go home, but she couldn't. She wouldn't leave until she saw Anthony Zorr again. She tried to focus on each well-wisher's face, but it was hard. Every time she saw the back of a shaggy blond head her heart leapt, only to plunge as soon as she caught a glimpse of the face.

It was never his.

Where was he? Marni Lamb had to be here. Sherri Winestine and Benji had already stopped by, name-dropping their clients.

Here came Frank.

She rested her free hand on his shoulder and kissed each of his cheeks. "Thank you for the diamonds and for sending Mel and Lynn."

"They do a great job, and the necklace, it looks stunning. How are you holding up?"

"I'm trying to convince myself this isn't a dream."

He pointed to the award. "When you wake up in the morning, and it's still on your nightstand, you'll know it was real."

She laughed.

"Can I get you a refill?" he asked.

"No, thank you. After last night, I need to slow down. The Marais—whatever—was delicious, but I drank too much of it."

It was one of the reasons she had to see Anthony. All day she'd puzzled over her extreme reaction to him. Kerrin half-feared, half-hoped alcohol had embellished her memory of his beautiful and dangerous perfection.

"Have you seen Marni Lamb tonight?" she asked.

"Colossal Talent's party is at the Blue Towers," Frank said.

Blue Towers was one of the better kept secrets in Glitter City. Kerrin often met Joanie and Norah in the lobby bar. The drinks and gourmet nuts were the best in town, but it was on the other side of town. Kerrin's keyed-up anticipation nosedived.

"Have any projects in the pipeline?" Frank asked.

"Nothing solid," she said.

"Let me send you the *Demion Glass* script."

"Sure."

"I think you'll like it," Frank said. "It's got depth."

"I like depth."

"I know you do. I've watched all your movies. That's why I thought of you."

"I'm sure I'll love it." What if she didn't?

Up until now, Kerrin had never accepted a script unless it felt like she'd die if someone else directed it. And a man possessed by a demon—ugh! She envisioned buckets of fake blood.

Her gaze ping-ponged around the large hall, taking in her competition. How much of herself would she compromise to move up the next rung of the ladder?

It was an uncomfortable question.

Frank moved closer and put his arm around her.

She stopped breathing.

"I'd love for your next project to be with us," he said. "You're talented. You deserve a studio film. Big budget. Special effects. Great costumes. The hottest stars."

Special effects had ruined more decent scripts than bad actors, but she couldn't say that. "I'd love the opportunity."

"I've heard it's not the first one."

A spot in her gut burned. The fire engulfed her belly. Jim Gordon hadn't offered her an opportunity. The head of Super Big Budget studios had tried to get her on the casting couch like some young starlet, just because she'd made one mistake years ago.

A drunk Jenna Lee grabbed Frank's free arm. "Frankie," she cooed. "I've been looking all over for you. What are you doing?"

"Hoping that Kerrin and I are discussing her next project."

Jenna was now draped over Frank, who'd released Kerrin. "You promised you wouldn't talk business tonight, Frankie Baby."

Was she gurgling?

"He always talks business," Jenna said in a loud whisper. "That's all he talks about." She rubbed his stomach. Like

Buddha?

Frank Gianopoulos was sixty-something. Jenna couldn't be a day over 29. Kerrin caught herself. Who was she to judge?

"You don't mind if I steal him away, do you, Kerrin?"

She was surprised Jenna remembered her name.

"Oh, my gosh!" Jenna squealed.

Kerrin looked for piglets.

"That choker looks so fab on you. I told him it would."

Kerrin coughed. "You told him—"

"Every year, he signs the Director of the Year. It's his thing." Jenna swayed around Frankie Baby.

He tried to say something, but the young blonde actually shushed him with a finger to his lips. "I told him to send the choker and the hair and makeup folks. Did you love them?"

Bemused, Kerrin nodded. "They arrived at just the right moment."

"Oh, let me see your shoes." Jenna leaned over, her face parallel to the ground. "Lynn texted me a pic."

Kerrin raised the hem of her gown.

"They are so totally awesome! Where did you get them?"

"They were my grandmother's. She wore them on her wedding day."

"I want a pair just like for my wedding, Frankie."

"You two are engaged?" Kerrin asked.

"It's not common knowledge yet," he said.

"We didn't want the engagement party to be overshadowed by the awards show," Jenna said.

"Congratulations," Kerrin said. She'd never been so sincere or relieved. Jenna Lee wasn't going to let Frankie Baby try to bone her. "You know, Jenna's right, Frank. We really shouldn't be talking shop tonight."

"See-wee," Jenna chucked Frankie Baby's chin.

Baby talk.

Welcome to Glitter City.

§§§

"After the girl won the contest, so many people crowded around her that she couldn't see the boy."

"Was he hiding from her?"

Kerrin's stomach knotted. "No, he was with someone else."

"Another girl? Was she pretty?"

"No and no. It wasn't another girl, and she wasn't pretty at all."

"Then why did he go with her?" Mibi asked.

"Because she was a witch, and she'd cast a spell over him."

"Was it the Wicked Witch of the West?"

"No, it was the Wicked Witch of Iowa."

"Did she have a wart on the end of her nose?"

"She had an enormous wart and she was as square as a refrigerator."

"Mommy, refrigerators are rectangles."

Kerrin blinked. "What did you say?"

"Refrigerators aren't squares, they're rectangles."

"Right. She was like a refrigerator with a huge purple–"

"Orange!"

"–Orange wart on the end of her nose."

Mibi laughed.

Kerrin did, too. Almost ten years later, she could.

§§§

While she waited for the limo, Kerrin pulled out her cell phone to check the time. 12:34 am. Would Marni and Anthony still be at the Blue Towers party?

She pulled up the internet. Reception was decent. She Googled Marni Lamb and got a phone number for Colossal Talent. Kerrin put a call through to the agency. An answering service picked up.

"I need to leave a message for Marni Lamb."

"Is this an emergency?"

Kerrin hesitated. "It's a business emergency." She gave her number.

Her limo, a courtesy of Golden Pinnacle to all the nominees, pulled up to the curb. The driver got out to open her door. He'd barely closed it before her cell phone rang.

"Hello."

"I knew you'd win," Marni said.

"Thanks for returning my call so quickly."

"We're always available at Colossal Talent."

"Anthony Zorr—"

"I knew you'd love him. Lunch tomorrow at The Oak?"

"Yes. Uhm, Marni, will you… "

"I wouldn't dream of coming alone. Anthony will join us."

Kerrin broke into a smile. He was available for her. "Great. Thank you." She tapped the toe of her grandmother's rhinestone pump against the floorboard.

The night was full of magic.

§§§

"The girl really wanted to save the boy from the witch," Kerrin said.

Mibi smiled. "That was nice of her."

"Brave."

"I want to be brave."

Kerrin settled her hand on her daughter's chest. "Listen to your heart. That's what brave people do."

"But sometimes I listen to my heart, and I get in trouble. You and Daddy get mad at me."

Kerrin leaned back, so she was right next to her daughter. "Tell me when that happens. We'll talk about it."

Mibi wrapped four of her fingers around her mother's index finger. "I'll try to remember to do that."

Chapter 3: Queen Nessity

The next day, United Speed delivered the *Demion Glass* script to Kerrin's front door at 10:00 am. Whatever else Frank had done last night, he hadn't forgotten to send it.

Kerrin returned to her ritual breakfast. Green tea and a slice of Ezekiel toast spread thick with butter.

She dropped the package on the table and stared at it.

After her last bite of toast, she wiped her hands. Buttery thumb and finger prints would only make a mess of the pages. It wouldn't make crap writing easier to swallow. Kerrin pushed away her empty plate and pulled the box toward her.

Frank was head of one of the biggest studios in Glitter City. He wanted *Demion Glass* produced. She was his first choice for director. Yes, it was fetishistic that he had a thing for deflowering the Golden Pinnacle Best Director of the Year, but everyone had their issues.

As long as the deflowering didn't become literal.

Kerrin had confidence in Jenna Lee; it wouldn't.

The truth was: Directing a big budget film for a major studio was the prize Kerrin had been lusting after for years, and one guy's neurotic belt-notching didn't amount to much of a deterrent.

The real issue would be the script. Would she love it?

She swiveled around to grab a knife. It was almost 11:00 am. She was meeting Marni and Anthony for lunch at 2:00 pm.

Kerrin pried open the envelope and squared the pages in front of her.

Bright interior light. Demion Glass observes his wife, Elise Glass, through an exterior window. Unaware of his gaze, she digs even troughs in the frozen winter ground of their small courtyard, a sack of tulip bulbs at her side. His cell phone rings. He doesn't take his eyes from Elise as he pulls it from his pocket.

A silky voice greets him.

Demion's face transforms as he turns away from his wife and arranges to meet his mistress. Fade to shadow.

Outside snow begins to fall. A white halo of powder crowns Elise's head.

Immersed in the story, Kerrin continued to flip the pages. This wasn't a horror flick at all, it was a character study.

She pushed the script away and closed her eyes, allowing herself to absorb the story's impact. It was the twist. The psychological play on the demon. Some of the dialogue was strange, falling off beat as it did, but most of it was crisp. She could definitely do something with this script. It was fantastic.

Kerrin checked her cell phone.

1:15 pm! No time to wash her hair!

Water drummed on her shower cap and bare body. What to wear to lunch?

Before running out the door, Kerrin checked herself in the full-length hall mirror. Her hair, pulled back into a loose pony tail, left some wisps to frame her face. Compared to last night, her skin was bare. She'd never considered plastic surgery or any of the injectable fillers, but, honestly, she didn't need to. Her white linen shirt made the blue of her eyes look brighter, her worn, low-rise jeans showed off her lean legs and flat stomach.

She'd chosen a pair of short gladiator sandals, the faux leather as soft as gloves.

Everything about the image in the mirror depicted a woman at ease with herself.

It hadn't always been that way.

Kerrin banished those memories to a never-never place in her mind.

§§§

"The girl discovered the witch had locked the boy up in a place where no one else could find him."

"Where was that?"

Kerrin stood up and reached toward the ceiling. "In a big, huge gigantic oak tree."

Mibi sat straight up, her eyes glistening. "How did she get inside to rescue him?"

"There were guards," Kerrin said. "You had to give them a

key."

"Where did she find a key?"

"She carved one out of wood."

Mibi frowned. "That girl must be smarter than me. I would never have thought of making a key myself."

Kerrin returned to the bed and gave her daughter a hug. "You'd be surprised what you can come up with when necessity demands it."

"Who's Nessity?"

Kerrin smiled. "A queen who rules the borders between the Enchanted World and the real one."

"Is she mean?"

"She can be, but most of the time she just makes us dig deeper, and when we dig deeper, we find gold."

"Queen Nessity sounds like my math teacher. Whenever I tell her I can't do a problem, she doesn't believe me."

§§§

The Oak was where you ate lunch when you wanted everyone in Glitter City to know who you were eating lunch with.

"Do you have a reservation?" the maître'd asked.

"I'm with the Marni Lamb party."

"Right this way."

The restaurant was packed. Not surprising the day after the Golden Pinnacle awards. Kerrin sauntered behind The Oak's maître'd, confident. Producers, agents, actors, people she knew—and didn't—waved. A few stopped her to offer congratulations.

Anthony stood up before she reached the table. Had Marni prompted him? Her lower abdomen tingled. It hadn't been the champagne. The man was gorgeous. Daylight, dim light, she suspected that beneath any light, his face begged for film. Tape me. Snap me. Take me. From every angle.

Kerrin's heart fluttered.

Forty-eight hours earlier, she'd had nothing. Today, she had everything. That was Glitter City.

She ordered the Caesar salad with grilled salmon. He had a burger—free range beef—and fries.

Marni tucked into a thin crust gourmet pizza. Vegan. "Would you like to try a slice?" she asked Kerrin. "It's to die for."

"Salmon's filling. I don't think I'll have room."

"Got to watch your figure."

Kerrin nodded. Yes, or I'll become a geometric shape like you.

"Anthony has a healthy appetite," Marni said. "He ate a slice of pizza before you got here."

"Charming," Kerrin said. Marni was a food pusher.

"Perhaps a glass of red wine?" the woman asked.

"Please."

Marni poured it herself. "Thatta girl."

God, she was irritating. If Anthony wasn't so perfect, Kerrin would have knocked the full glass in Marni's lap, apologized, and left.

While they finished their meals, Kerrin made every effort to draw Anthony into the conversation, but he was reticent. Some of the best actors were. Unless they were on stage, speaking from a script, they fell silent, observing the humanity around them, drawing details and eccentricities to create unforgettable performances.

Anthony's blue eyes studied the room. Kerrin wished Marni would go to the bathroom. Despite drinking almost the entire bottle of wine herself, the woman remained wedged in her seat.

"Have you read the Demion Glass script?" Marni asked.

"Almost finished," Kerrin hedged.

"Don't you think Anthony's perfect for the part?"

"I can see him as Demion."

"Others have expressed interest in the role?" Marni asked.

Anthony was attentive to their conversation, but didn't interject.

"You know how it is," Kerrin said. "You win a Golden Pinnacle, and everyone comes calling."

"Who's come calling?" Marni asked.

Kerrin focused on a bite a salmon.

"Demion needs to be young!" Marni exclaimed. "James Fellowes, King Wentworth, and Bruce Rik are too old."

Two out of three. Impressive. The woman did her research. "A younger Demion could capitalize on innocence," Kerrin acknowledged.

"Exactly." Marni's flat palm slapped the table. "The less experience the better."

Her emphatic agreement awoke an urge to argue just for the sake of opposing the woman. "And yet," Kerrin said, "if the actor were more seasoned, breaking through a cynical exterior could make for a compelling dramatic climax."

Marni folded her fingers in half. "You want your first major studio film to be a smash at the box office. It needs to hit the right demographics. Old people don't go out to the movies anymore, and teenagers and twenty-somethings don't want to spend their Friday nights watching someone their father's age have an epiphany."

She had a point. "Have you heard when the screen tests will be scheduled?" Kerrin needled. Frank's administrative assistant would have shared that information if she'd taken Marni's call.

Marni glanced away. "Soon." When she turned back to Kerrin, a clownish smile plastered her face. "More wine?" Marni picked up the bottle then set it down. "You haven't even touched your first glass. Well, I've had more than one. I need to hit the powder room." The woman almost knocked the table over as she pushed her chair away.

Relieved to be alone with Anthony, Kerrin asked him if he'd read the script.

He soaked a French fry in ketchup. "Not a big reader."

If this were an indie project, she'd have grilled his nonchalance on the spot, but Frank hadn't officially hired her. It wasn't the right time to press.

"What are you big on?" she asked.

"The ladies."

She didn't doubt that, and yet, there was that bashful grin again. She couldn't repress her own smile. His frank charm appealed. "I'm guessing they're big on you, too."

"There are lot of beautiful women in Glitter City," he conceded. "And I'm sitting across the table from one of them."

Did he just lick the ketchup off his French fry?

The tremulous feelings in her chest and abdomen met at her ribcage. She settled her elbow on the table and her cheek in her palm.

He dangled another French fry in the bright red ketchup, spun it around, then held it up to her. "These are the best damned French fries I've ever eaten."

Kerrin accepted his offering. The cool ketchup coated a crunchy exterior that exploded into a burst of soft, interior flavor. Spontaneous delight spilled out as a giggle. She felt like she was fifteen years younger and had never known Tom. The intrusive thought unsettled her. She shifted in her seat and brushed her lips with her napkin.

"It's good isn't it?" he asked.

"Delicious," she said, but the joy had left her voice. Deep chasms gaped on both sides of the inner wall she balanced upon.

"I'd feed them to you." He glanced around. "If everyone wasn't staring at us."

Kerrin made her own assessment of The Oak's patrons. Her face heated up. Everyone was staring in their direction. Surreptitiously, covertly, openly, the room's attention was on them. No, it wasn't—this couldn't be—about Tom.

She needed to let it go and return her focus to Anthony. "The best actors are magnets for the limelight," she said.

"They're not looking at me," he said. "You were glowing."

The key word being *were*. She tried to recapture the playful mood that memories of Tom had deflated. "Must be the effect of sleeping with the Golden Pinnacle last night."

A meteor of enthusiasm burst across his face. "Did you really sleep with it? Like hold it in your arms?"

She laughed. It was genuine if shaky. "No, it remained primly on my nightstand."

"Then you were alone last night?" he asked.

The tart comeback her mind scrambled for eluded her.

"That's sad," he said.

Her throat constricted. What was Marni doing in the bathroom? Taking a shower?

"Not really."

"Where I come from, a beautiful lady, such as yourself,

would never have to spend such a special night alone."

"You're quite the charmer," she said.

"That makes me sound insincere."

"I didn't mean—"

He reached across the table. "Will you spend tonight alone?"

She jerked her hand away.

"You need to celebrate," he said. "Those Glitter City parties don't count. They're too much like work."

"I—" She didn't know which was worse: that she didn't want to say no or that she couldn't.

"I'll come by your place at 10:00." He slid his phone in her direction. "Where is it?"

By the time Marni returned, Kerrin had typed her private address into Anthony's contacts.

"Everything settled?" Marni asked.

"Lunch was great," Anthony said. "I like this place."

§ § §

"Did the girl give the guards the key?" Mibi asked.

"Yes, she did."

"Did they let her go inside the oak tree and see the boy?"

"She had to eat dinner with the witch first."

"Was it awful?"

"Toad's eyes, snake's bellies, pond scum, and rotted boar's hooves."

"Eww. That's so gross. Did it make her sick?"

"It gave her nightmares."

"What kind of nightmares?"

That was good a question.

§ § §

Lights flashed when Kerrin walked outside, Anthony beside her.

Her jaws and shoulders tensed. Over twenty years ago, she'd been the next big thing, and a single indiscretion had turned her world upside down. Young and vulnerable, the paparazzi had made her life a living hell.

Her hands shook when she handed the valet her ticket.

They shouted her name. They yelled questions. They congratulated her on her Golden Pinnacle award. She steeled her insides.

How long before they resurrected the summer with Tom?

She could hardly look at Anthony to say goodbye. Marni stood silently behind them. Strange behavior from someone so adamantly vocal. An odd wave of nausea seized Kerrin.

Those had been challenging years—the Tom year, the one preceding it, and the two following.

Hannah had passed away the summer before Kerrin's senior year. It had been rough, losing her grandmother and being left to deal with her mother, who daily spiraled deeper into some unreachable abyss. Despite her lifetime of antagonism toward Hannah, Emery hadn't taken her mother's death well. The primary target of her rage had been Kerrin's future. She swore up and down her daughter didn't have one any brighter than hers, and she was a fool if she thought that she did. Hannah should never have given her that camera.

That spring, there had been a notice for extras on the drama department bulletin board. Kerrin had been ecstatic. She applied, making it clear she preferred work as an intern or assistant to the crew, rather than as an extra. She'd been hired as a gofer.

The director, Tom Barnes, had taken an immediate liking to her. When he realized how much she knew about lighting, he began letting her hang around for takes. They hired someone else to run the errands.

Kerrin had learned the script by heart. When the lead actress came down with the flu, rather than halt production,

Tom asked her to stand in; they could film scenes around Kerrin. She'd stepped in without a second thought. Tom had been encouraging, and knowing her takes would never see the light of day, it had been easy to relax.

One evening he'd invited her to watch some of the dailies. He raved that she was a natural; the camera loved her.

When Tom and the crew packed up and left town, Kerrin had drifted, uncertain what to do with her life. There was no money to go to film school, or any school. The industry was tough, and Kerrin didn't know if she was ready for a film career without credentials. She missed Tom and his professional camaraderie.

When he called her out of the blue and offered to fly her to Glitter City for a job, it had felt like a hand had reached down from heaven and pulled her out of hell. She hadn't thought beyond her escape and getting a real job in the industry.

What had caught her off guard was Tom's offer to have her play the lead in his next film. A pattern of friendly lunches became friendly dinners. Some part of her had known they were getting too close. More than twenty years her senior, he was married and had a family. The rumors about them having an affair had started well before they ever crossed the line. In

47

the end, it had been one night, but the pictures before and after their rendezvous made it appear like much more.

Tom and his wife divorced. The tabloids accused Kerrin of being a home wrecker. Glossy photos of Tom's two young children were always front and center. Kerrin had felt strangely hollow and numb. The press junket had been a blur, but the film became a huge critical and commercial success.

Kerrin had shaved her head and enrolled in film school. The hefty check from her film role financed her Associate Degree in Video Production. By the time she graduated, it became clear that she had an eye for intriguing stories, and a talent for making them come to life. With her portfolio, she'd begun the arduous journey of selecting scripts and seeking financial backing. One script, one film, one budget at a time, she'd built her reputation. But there hadn't been much time for love or family. A few relationships, but nothing lasting.

Kerrin put on her sunglasses and slipped into the driver's seat. Irrational fear awakened her personal demons. Memories of a world spinning out-of-control in the blinding lights blotted out the present.

The irony of her directing a movie about a man becoming psychotic rather than face the guilt over a sexual affair hit too close to home.

§ § §

"The girl had nightmares about a king," Kerrin said.

"Was he a mean, bad king?"

"Not mean or bad. Full of sorrow, I think."

"Sad kings aren't scary," Mibi said.

But they can still inflict untold damage. "They are when they cry so many tears they drown the world."

"The whole entire world?"

"That was the nightmare. The king cried and cried and cried until the entire world flooded."

"I don't know if I believe you," Mibi said.

"Remember, it was a nightmare, and nightmares never stand up to the light of day."

"Okay, but I think the story would be better if he was a mad king—or a crazy king."

Chapter 4: The Spiral Staircase

At 10:00 pm on the dot, someone knocked on Kerrin's door. Her pulse pounded in her ears. It had to be Anthony. She wasn't expecting anyone else. Still in jeans, but now wearing a sweat shirt and socks, she padded through the entryway, slow and ambivalent, her body, mind, and soul a conflicted triangle.

It had been a long evening of taking stock. Her conclusion: The greater the public acclaim for her professional achievements, the more treacherous the need-sucking undertow to be cherished and loved for no particular reason at all. Unfortunately, acknowledging that vulnerability did

nothing to temper her curiosity—or her desire. If anything, it heightened the craving to relinquish control.

Just for the night.

She stopped. One night. That's all it would take to bring her world crashing down around her again.

Kerrin leaned against the wall.

The doorbell chimed.

Why hadn't she called Norah or Joanie?

She pushed a stray hair behind her ears and wiped at her eyes with the back of her hand. She hadn't called her friends because Kerrin didn't confess her sins. She buried them deep.

Kerrin glanced at herself in the mirror. Her makeup was gone. Pink tinged her eyelids. She admitted careless grooming was a flimsy barrier against self-destruction, but it was the best she could manage on short notice.

She checked the peep hole. He was so goddamned beautiful.

What game was she playing? Anthony Zorr was dangerous. The knowing pulsed through her entire body. It wouldn't be long before the tabs were paying thousands of dollars for photos of him, and every secret he'd ever wanted to hide. The paparazzi would sniff him out like bitches in heat. If she became his secret, could she survive another detonation?

Feeling reckless, she unlocked the door.

He waved a bottle of wine. "Evening, ma'am."

She opened the door wider. "Punctual."

He had on jeans, a jacket, and those flip-flops. His shaggy-blond hair half-covered his eyes. The night air shimmered around him. His very presence on her doorstep seemed untrustworthy.

"You gonna' keep me standing here all night?"

"Come in." She got a whiff of leather, aftershave, and pot. Hormones pounded her blood. She closed the door and shoved her hands deep into the pockets of her jeans. A physical reminder to keep them to herself.

He didn't wait for her as he strode down the hall toward the brightest source of light, the kitchen, adjacent to her informal screening room. A large flat screen TV hooked up to her computer.

Kerrin padded after him, tingling from head to toe. She couldn't remember the last time she'd felt such intense physical attraction to someone.

He set the wine bottle on the table. "Thirsty?"

"I wouldn't mind a glass of–"

"Cabernet Sauvignon."

Just the sound of his voice set off spirals of pleasure. She opened a cabinet and reached for two wine glasses.

His arms circled her waist.

Kerrin froze. If she said nothing, he'd interpret that as a yes. If she pulled away, pushed him away, the familiar easiness he took for granted would evaporate.

He nuzzled the back of her neck.

Wine glasses in hand, Kerrin steadied her wrists against the counter. Every cell in her body was aware of him. It had been too long since anyone had touched her like this.

He pulled her body closer to him.

He was moving too fast. She ducked beneath his arm and hurried to the table and the bottle of wine. Damn. She needed the wine opener. Could she make it to the drawer without another awkward dance?

War raged between her mind and body. The visceral desire to surrender urged her to stop thinking. Enough with the critical analysis! Take the leap!

Indeed, why had she agreed to let a man she hardly knew come over to her home at 10:00 at night? What had she expected they would do?

Her protective shell struggled to regain the upper hand.

This a really bad idea! The worst one you've had in years!

Her eyes settled on the *Demion Glass* script stacked neatly on the table. She longed to discuss Demion with him.

He followed her gaze. "Marni says it's a great script."

"But you haven't read it yourself?" she asked.

"Like I said, not much of a reader."

Kerrin needed some air—breathing space to decide: Was she going to make this about being Kerrin Mayham, the Director, and Anthony Zorr, the Actor? Or was she going to make this about her body and his and cross a line she swore she'd never cross again?

He folded his arms across his chest and smiled that compelling smile.

She took advantage of his stationary position and edged toward the drawer where she kept the wine opener.

"So, how do you know Marni?" Kerrin asked.

"My mom."

"Your mother?"

"Marni's from Iowa. She and my mom go way back. Marni's known me since I was a baby. It's a little embarrassing. She wanted to bring me out to Glitter City sooner, but Mom wouldn't let her."

Kerrin absorbed that information. "You're lucky to have a connection like that. Colossal Talent is one of the most prestigious talent agencies in the business."

He gave her one of those *aw, shucks* grins as she handed him a glass of wine. She wondered if everything in his life had come as easy.

"So your family's well off?" she asked.

He shrugged. "Comparatively."

"Compared to what?"

"Compared to everyone else in the hick town I'm from, but not compared to people who are well off here."

She didn't doubt that. The well off in Glitter City did better than the well off anywhere else in the world.

"Girlfriend back home?" Kerrin asked.

He took a sip of wine. "A few broken hearts." He averted his gaze. "And other things."

Maybe he referred to friendships. No post-adolescent male would want Anthony as a wingman. "I can imagine."

"Can you?"

The question could have been arrogant, but that's not how

she took it. He said it as though he didn't know he was beautiful and dangerous. Like he was relieved that she believed he could have broken a few hearts and other things.

Kerrin studied him. Actors were so hard to read. Sometimes they didn't even know when they were playing a role. Feeding off the energy around them and giving the person standing across from them exactly what they needed and wanted.

Was that what he was doing with her?

She rubbed her finger across her lip. If he'd told the truth about his age, she was thirteen years older. Strange that the age gap didn't feel like the chasm she would have expected it to be.

"Yeah," Kerrin said, suddenly realizing she'd left his question, his need for assurance, hanging in the air between them. "I don't normally do this," she said.

"Do what?" he asked.

"Audition actors in my home late at night." She wanted to take back the words as soon as she'd said them.

"It's not that late," he said. The digital clock read 10:44 pm. "Besides I didn't come over here tonight for an audition," he said.

"No?"

"You're beautiful," he said.

Was she blushing? Damn. She couldn't remember the last time someone had told her that. And certainly no one had ever said it so unequivocally, with so much conviction—lust, she reminded herself—in his voice. The effect was intoxicating.

He walked up to her, took her empty wine glass, and set it on the table. He cupped his hands around her neck. Again, his touch was electric and welcome. He leaned toward her and brushed her lips with his.

This wasn't going to end well.

But she couldn't stop it.

He'd unlocked a dam inside her, and the torrential roar drowned everything else out.

§§§

"So what about the boy?" Mibi asked. "Did the girl rescue him from the oak tree?"

"She tried."

Mibi banged the backs of her hands against her knee. "She failed?"

"When she found him at the bottom of a long spiral staircase that went deep below ground, he didn't want to leave."

"Why not? Wasn't it dark and scary down there?"

"It was very dark and very scary. Spiders and snakes lived down there, and there were lots of bones, stripped clean of meat. But the witch's enchantment was so strong, the boy could convince himself that he lived in a glorious meadow next to a babbling brook warmed by the sun—if he wanted to."

"Did he want to?"

"Sometimes, but sometimes he didn't. Sometimes he liked being in that dark, ugly place."

"She should have left him there if he liked it even a little bit."

§§§

The next morning clanking sounds woke Kerrin. They were coming from the kitchen. She reached for the top drawer of her nightstand. Before she pulled it open, she remembered. Anthony Zorr.

Was he making breakfast?

She curled back down into her bed. He'd been wonderful. Attentive, passionate, fun. She kicked off the covers and picked up his t-shirt from the floor. She pulled it over her head and tiptoed down the hall.

"Pancakes?" she asked.

Shirtless, he came over and kissed her on the mouth. "Need

to put some meat on those bones. Nice shirt."

"Is that what they say in Iowa?" she asked.

He looked confused. "Nice shirt?"

"No, 'need to put some meat on those bones'?"

"That? Oh yeah, all the chubby mothers say that to all the young, skinny girls. It's like they don't want to stop feeding them until they lose their figures, too."

Kerrin raised her eyebrows. "So that's where Marni gets it."

Anthony laughed as he turned off the stove, shuffled some dishes and utensils around, then settled a plate with pancakes, scrambled eggs, and two strips of bacon on the table. "For you," he said.

"Where's yours?"

"I've already eaten. I've got to meet a trainer at 9:00. Marni hooked me up with him. Wouldn't look good to be late to my first appointment."

So he had a thing for being on time.

He pulled out her chair and kissed her before she sat down.

Where had he disappeared to? A few seconds later he came back, trailing her bed sheet. He leaned over and whispered in her ear, "Trade you for my shirt."

She pulled it off, feeling the heat rise in her cheeks.

He wrapped her in the sheet. "I'll let myself out and lock the door behind me. Enjoy breakfast."

Disheartened by his abrupt departure, Kerrin stared at her plate of food with no appetite.

She pushed it away, folded her arms on the table, and cradled her head in them.

§§§

"The girl couldn't bear to leave the boy in the dark, ugly place because he was so beautiful."

"She stayed down there with him?"

"Yes."

"Was that wrong?" Mibi asked.

"Sometimes things aren't wrong or right, honey. Sometimes they just are what they are."

"But wasn't it dangerous for her to be down there in the dark with all those spiders and snakes and bones?"

"It was very dangerous."

"I don't care how beautiful he was, I would have left him down there," her daughter said.

That would have been the smart thing to do.

§§§

Kerrin took a long, hot bath. She submerged herself.

Had last night been worth it? She couldn't find a *no* anywhere inside her.

As she towel-dried her hair, Kerrin checked her cell. Norah. Marni. What did she want? Joanie. Frankie Baby. Her insides zinged. That was the call she'd been waiting for. Joanie had called a second time.

Kerrin went to make a pot of green tea. Ritual always centered her. She sliced the fresh ginger root and dumped it into the electric kettle. When the tea was done, she scooted out to her tiny oriental garden. Even though her backyard was minuscule, she'd hired a landscape architect to create the serene environment as soon as she'd closed on the house four years earlier.

The garden's symmetry soothed her and helped her think.

Kerrin set down her tea cup and said a prayer to whatever gods might be benevolently disposed toward her this morning. She pulled up Frank's call and pushed redial.

"Kerrin," he answered the phone.

His private number. Her stomach did a little flip.

"Have you had a chance to read the *Demion Glass* script?" he asked.

"You were right. I love it."

"Good," he said. "When can you get down to the studio to talk legalese and numbers?"

She struggled to find the right note. Anytime sounded too easy. "My work schedule's pretty wide open." That sounded better. She'd already told him she didn't have any other projects lined up, and it threw the ball back in his court.

"This afternoon at five?"

"See you then."

A late afternoon appointment would give her time to get to the gym and decompress. She ran her fingers along the edge of her phone. When was she going to tell Norah and Joanie about last night? The longer she kept them in the dark, the more pissed off they were going to be.

But she wasn't ready to talk about Anthony yet. For now, she wanted to keep him to herself.

Her little secret.

§§§

"How long did she stay down there with him?" Mibi asked.

"Too long."

"What happened?"

"One day she heard the click-clack of the witch's boots

against the stairs."

Mibi shook her body in an exaggerated shiver. "What happened when the witch caught the girl with the boy?"

"She laughed an awful laugh. It sounded like a screech. The girl had to cover her hands with her ears."

"Did it sound like fingernails against a chalkboard?"

"That's exactly what it sounded like."

Chapter 5: A Single Question

Glenda buzzed Kerrin into Frank's office.

He gestured to the conference table that took up half the enormous room.

"Did Glenda offer you something to drink?" he asked, before returning his attention to his computer screen.

"Yes, I told her I'm fine."

He nodded.

When he was finished with whatever he was doing on the computer, he poked his head out the door. "Glenda, send the guys from Finance and Legal up with the contracts in about thirty minutes." Frank pulled out the chair next to Kerrin and swiveled to face her. "So you're going to do it?"

"I'm very interested," she said.

"What are your bottom lines?"

Now, she wished she'd asked Glenda for a bottle of water. Taking a few sips would have given her time to think without making her look like she didn't know what in the hell she was doing, a feeling Kerrin hated.

Bringing Jonas, her attorney, to this first meeting hadn't occurred to her. It should have. Frank had told her they were going to discuss legal issues. She made a stab in the dark. "Final approval on the cast and script."

Frank ran his palm across his forehead. "Come on, Kerrin, that's every director's bottom line. You need to push harder. Give me something I haven't heard before."

His response disconcerted her. If she had control over the cast and the words they spoke, she could make anything work. What in the hell did he want her to say?

"Why don't you give me the boilerplate and I'll go over it with my attorney?"

"Yeah, all right." He didn't sound pleased with her response.

There was one other thing. "Are you envisioning filming here in the city?" she asked.

Frank tilted his head. "I'm not hiring you to fulfill my vision."

Of course, he wasn't. "I haven't been able to stop thinking about the script." Kind of a lie. But she had been thinking about it ever since Anthony had left. At the gym, on the treadmill, she'd begun to configure scenes and settings in her head. "I'd love to film the whole thing on location."

"No sets," he said.

"Here, in Glitter City."

"Can you control the costs?"

Controlling costs were what indie directors did. Every dime for a piece of bubblegum had to be counted. "I have a crew. I'd like to use them. If I use them, I guarantee I can control the costs."

Frank pulled out his smartphone and typed. "Cast, script, film crew—the studio will fill in any gaps there, location. Anything else?"

he'd spent too much of her afternoon in an Anthony-haze and not enough time prepping for this meeting! Her laugh was nervous. "What else is there?"

He swept his hand across the conference table. "Craft services, sound, final cuts, promotion–"

"I get it," she said. "I'm good."

"When can you start working with the location scout?" Frank asked.

"As soon as possible."

"I like it."

One point in her favor.

"Any ideas on the casting?" he asked.

She wanted to see Anthony's screen test without appearing biased. "I'd like to meet with the Casting Director to discuss my concept for each character. I'm happy to let him do his job, but I want to see all the screen tests."

Marni would make sure Anthony's audition was scheduled. As long as Kerrin saw it, and he filmed as well as she hoped he would, there shouldn't be any problems.

No problems besides the fact that she'd slept with him.

"I'll make sure Casting gets a memo," Frank said.

§§§

"When the girl thought her eardrums were going to burst, the witch stopped her horrible laughter."

"Ouch," Mibi said.

"Then the witch leaned over. She was so close to the girl that her orange wart almost touched the girl's nose."

"If it had, would it have burned all her skin off?"

"Most definitely."

"Did the girl back away?"

"She couldn't, her back was already against the wall."

§ § §

When Kerrin left Frank's office, her insides were on fire.

She was going to be able to throw all her creative energies into directing the film, while Frank, the producer, handled the budget, the hiring, the scheduling, and all the other tedious responsibilities she hated. Kerrin wanted to celebrate.

But Anthony hadn't called or texted.

She checked the time. It wasn't too late to make dinner plans with Norah and Joanie.

An hour later, Kerrin sipped a margarita and smiled into Joanie's smartphone. She couldn't believe she'd let them talk her into putting on the goofy, oversized sombrero. All three of them laughed as they passed the enormous hat around and took turns snapping pictures, while their waiter blessed them with generous patience.

Norah and Joanie had grilled her about the meeting with

Frank, but Kerrin had yet to mention Anthony.

She kept checking her phone. It was difficult to admit how disappointed she felt about Anthony's silence. Maybe it was why she was drinking too much tequila and trying too hard to have a good time with her friends.

What if Marni didn't deliver Anthony's screen test for the part of Demion? Could she let him go?

For the thousandth time that day, Kerrin cursed herself for not getting out her old Eklin last night and taking a few hundred black and whites of him.

"You okay?" Norah asked. "You look a little lost."

Kerrin took a gulp of margarita and wiped her mouth with the back of her hand. "Just thinking about locations."

"Well, I've got to get home and feed Boomer." Boomer was Joanie's golden lab.

"Sure, yeah," Kerrin said. "I need to get home, too."

"And do exactly what?" Norah asked.

"Call Jonas." She didn't really need to call her attorney as much as she needed to get him a copy of the contract the legal guy had slid across the conference room table this afternoon.

"Okay," Norah said.

"What about you?" Kerrin asked Norah.

"Tonight, it's going to be me and a good book."

Kerrin was hoping for something a little more exciting.

§ § §

"Was the girl trapped?" her daughter asked.

"The witch said she would let the girl go, and she could take the boy with her, if she could answer a single question correctly."

"What would happen if she answered the question wrong?"

"She'd have to stay at the bottom of the spiral staircase with the snakes and the spiders and the bones and the beautiful boy forever."

"Forever?"

"The witch held up her hands, her fingernails were like claws. 'Forever, and I'll scratch the beauty right off your face.'"

Mibi's chin dropped.

Kerrin worried she'd made the witch too scary tonight. She hoped her daughter didn't have nightmares.

§ § §

The sun had set. Hands filled with groceries, Kerrin was shutting her car door with her knee.

"Hey." The low voice growled from so close behind her hot

air hit her neck.

Kerrin shoved her elbow back in a defensive punch and ran toward her back door, praying the garden gate was unlatched. If it was, the gate's automatic lock would activate when she slammed it shut. It wouldn't stop anyone determined to get into her backyard, but it would buy her some time to get the door to the house unlocked.

She heard him jogging behind her, keeping up.

"Whoa. Careful there." That time the voice was familiar.

She whirled around. "Sneaking up on someone like that in the dark is not cool." Her heart pounded in her throat.

"Wow. I didn't know you were so jumpy," Anthony said.

"This isn't Iowa. A lot of creepy things happen in this city."

He held up his hands. "My bad."

She shook her head. "I wasn't expecting you. Next time, let me know you're coming over."

"I get it. Keep things formal," he said.

When had texting someone become formal? With her back to Anthony, Kerrin rolled her eyes while she unlocked the door. She dropped her keys and bag on the counter.

Anthony was right behind her.

The digital clock on the range read 10:25 pm.

Kerrin felt pissy. Anthony's assumption that he could come by without warning and take whatever he wanted didn't sit well with her. "I had a meeting with Frank today about directing *Demion Glass.*"

"Right on," he said.

She wondered if he called guys dudes.

"Have you had a chance to look at the script yet?" she asked.

"I stopped by Marni's this afternoon. She went over it with me."

"What does that mean?"

"You know, she told me when I needed to show up for my audition and stuff."

Kerrin raised her eyebrows.

He came toward her, put his hands on her hips, and kissed her.

He was playing her, but Kerrin didn't push him away. It was too late for that, her body was too needy. She let the delicious sense of surrender envelope her. She was going to get what she wanted, too.

§§§

"The witch told the girl she would be gone for seven days, and while she was gone, the girl was to watch the beautiful boy very carefully. When the witch returned, she would ask the girl what she'd seen."

"Was that a trick question?"

"Kind of."

"I don't like trick questions," Mibi said.

§§§

The next morning, Anthony was still asleep when Kerrin woke up. She tiptoed out of her bedroom and went to get the Eklin. Dispatching the ethics of snapping him without his permission —no one but her would ever see these photos—she eased back into the room and studied her subject.

The sheet covered his right leg. That was all. The lens zoomed in on his cheekbones, full bottom lip, and straight nose; the strong arch of his eyebrows scattered into wings at the outer edges; the coffee-with-cream colored skin; and his hair—streaked with bleach.

Kerrin dragged the camera from her eye. It was subtle, but she could tell it wasn't natural.

She readjusted the frame and clicked a few shots.

Last night had been good, but not as good as the night before. Kerrin considered the difference. The first night

Anthony had been present. Last night he had not.

She considered making him breakfast, but realized she'd rather go out. An impossibility unless she wanted to risk it showing up in some gossip magazine.

The reality of what she was doing settled in.

She'd let a much younger man, a stranger she knew very little about, into her private life without reservation.

Kerrin stepped out of the bedroom and padded down the hall, stopping in front of her full length mirror. Her long body was as trim as ever. The only blemishes on her skin were the results of age, a few dark splotches and an oddly placed freckle or mole. To her, they were barely visible, but what about to Anthony? What did he see when he looked at her?

Did he really see a beautiful, desirable woman? Or was Kerrin just a means to an end? A way to get one of the most coveted lead roles in Glitter City?

She dragged her fingers through her mane of hair. When she didn't get it blown out, it got wild and unruly. Kerrin liked it that way.

Did Anthony like it that way?

She tapped her finger against her lip.

She'd seen him with Marni, all *aw, shucks, Ma'am,* and with Frank, silently acquiescent to the alpha male. Kerrin got a slightly different word-minimal self, highly physical, but still— reflective.

A lot of actors were effortless chameleons, but it was like Anthony had zero center.

Kerrin shuddered.

There was something hollow about him.

Her cell phone went off, rattling against the kitchen counter where she'd dropped it last night. She raced down the hall, set the clunky Eklin down on the counter, and checked the number.

Norah.

Kerrin rubbed her forehead. She didn't answer her phone. Instead she sat down at her kitchen table and thought about Tom.

She'd been in awe of his technical brilliance. It had been too easy to let things go too far. But why had she let herself get carried away with Anthony? What good could come out of it?

Maybe she needed to talk to Joanie, the sex goddess.

Anthony poked his head into the kitchen. "Gotta run." He

was dressed. He didn't seem to notice she wasn't. "See you tonight?"

"Sure," she said.

Kerrin listened to his footsteps fade down the hall. She definitely needed to talk with Joanie.

Her cell buzzed again. "Marni, hi."

The Colossal Talent agent didn't waste time with pleasantries. She informed Kerrin that Anthony would be auditioning for the part of Demion Glass. Then she proceeded to tell Kerrin all the reasons he was the best actor for the part. None of them had to do with his acting ability.

"No, I won't be at the studio when the screen tests are shot, but they'll all be sent to me."

"Did Frank give you final approval on casting?" Marni asked.

Kerrin evaded. "We're hashing out the details now."

"If you get final approval, we both know you don't need a screen test."

WTF.

Indie directors had more control than directors on studio projects. Kerrin had always known that. It was the reason she'd never seriously entertained any of the feelers the studio heads had put out to her in the past, and why she'd waited to take on a project like *Demion Glass* when she had more leverage.

Her negotiations with Frank had validated her stubborn patience, and she wasn't about to squander that hard-won control on a complete unknown. Her recovered objectivity increased her irritation with Anthony's agent.

But the flames of adrenaline coursing through Kerrin's arms and legs weren't about what Marni had said. She was just doing her job. Whatever it took to get her client signed. If she could persuade Kerrin to bypass the screen tests, she'd effectively wipe out Anthony's competition.

Frank's studio might not churn out as many cheesy hits as Super Big Budget studios, but its vehicles were more critically acclaimed. For Marni, getting Anthony signed would be a sweet deal.

No, something else was surfacing infrared on Kerrin's radar. It was the tone in Marni's voice. Positively creepy.

"Thanks for bringing Anthony to my attention. I'm sure he'll film beautifully. I'll be in touch." Kerrin pushed End Call and stalked back to her bedroom.

She threw herself on her bed.

His smell and the smell of their sex engulfed her.

§§§

"The first day after the witch left them at the bottom of the spiral staircase, the girl stared at the boy."

"Did she see anything?"

"His eyebrows wiggled like two worms."

Mibi rolled on the bed and snorted, a sight that always made Kerrin's heart burst with joy.

Chapter 6: Snake Guts & Nails for Teeth

Kerrin and Anthony fell into a routine.

She spent her long days finalizing her contract with Frank's studio, hanging out with the location scout, marking up the script, meeting with the casting director and his assistant, and taking Glenda to lunch. Films were collaborative. When the time came to make critical decisions, being able to shift strategic support to your point of view was crucial. The more Frank's assistant trusted Kerrin, the smoother things would be.

Every night, between 9:30 and 11:00, Anthony showed up, and they had sex. He had a taste for drugs. They didn't improve his performance.

A few times Kerrin heard him fumbling around in her bathroom. She didn't care enough to ask him what in the hell he was doing. For all their physical wrangling, she felt distant from him, even though he always spent the night.

They never talked about *Demion Glass*.

Which Kerrin thought was strange. Any other actor would have pumped her for insight that would give him an edge on the screen test.

Not Anthony. It was all bashful grins and silencing kisses. And yet Kerrin sensed the young man fraying around the edges.

She'd never gotten around to talking about him with Joanie. The truth was she didn't know what she would say. I'm having hot, meaningless sex with the young god who has the inside track for the lead of my next film.

What could Joanie do, besides squeeze her for details, and tell her she was nuts?

When Kerrin woke up in the middle of the night, she thought about Tom. Had she loved him? Did it matter? Why hadn't she ever got gotten married, or started a family, or at least committed to a longterm relationship?

Emery's shadow lurked in the dark corners of Kerrin's bedroom.

But, that wasn't an answer. That was just Emery's legacy.

§§§

"The second day, the girl watched the boy even more carefully. He caught one of the snakes with his bare hands and squeezed it between his filthy fingers."

"Did the guts come out like jelly?" Mibi asked.

Kerrin wrinkled her nose. "Just like slimy Jello."

"Did he eat it?"

"He wanted the girl to eat it."

Mibi's brown eyes, the same color as her father's, grew round. "Did she?"

"No," Kerrin said. "She knew if she ate it, the witch would never let her leave, even if she answered the question correctly."

§§§

Kerrin's stomach twisted on the morning United Speed

83

delivered the screen tests. Everything had been neatly labeled in padded envelopes. One flash drive for each character. Mark Chisolm, the casting director's assistant, was an organized dream. She reminded herself to send him a bottle of vintage wine. From what she could tell, he did all the work while his boss got all the glory, and probably, took home a big, fat paycheck for doing the delegating.

That's how Glitter City worked. Interns and assistants worked their asses off, hoping to connect with the right people and the right opportunity.

There were more than forty tests for Demion. From a handful of unknowns to some of the most bankable names in the business, James Fellowes and Bruck Rik among them.

Kerrin hunkered down to watch.

Mark had made notations of each performance, critical assessments, but no rankings. After each shot, she made her own notes then studied his. Although he viewed elements of the auditions differently than she did, his observations were incisive.

Kerrin purposefully watched the clips in random order.

Her stomach twisted when she got to Anthony's test. She got up from the sofa and stretched. The black and whites she'd taken of him had exploded with the promise she'd anticipated. Some people's physical exteriors were made to film. Anthony was one of those people. Kerrin sat back down and pressed play.

The scene Mark had chosen for the screen test was one shared between Demion and his lover.

A young husband, passionately in love with his equally young and innocent wife, Elise, Demion allows himself to be seduced by a more sexually experienced woman, Sophia. From their first encounter, Sophia artfully and effectively taps into Demion's darkest desires. Desires he's unaware of until he meets her.

The scene required the actor to showcase the character's first internal shift.

Anthony sauntered on screen the same way he'd entered Kerrin's kitchen the first night he'd come to her house. Watching the duplicate performance gave her a chill. Things didn't improve. The aching beauty she'd captured in the stills wasn't present.

Why?

As Anthony approached the actress playing Sophia, Kerrin's stomach knotted. The bashful grin plastering his face transformed into a grotesque leer—a sense of *fuck you, cunt* seeped through the *aw, shucks* veneer. He delivered a few lines before Kerrin pressed stop.

What was so disturbing about what she'd just seen?

She hit rewind and watched again. It was the way he looked at Sophia. The camera caught a glint of empty coldness in his eyes.

Hollow.

She doubled over.

Either, he wasn't acting in the screen test, or he'd been acting every time he'd been with her.

Kerrin forced herself to finish watching the clip.

What came through on film wasn't his external beauty, but his interior ugliness. There was something monstrous about Anthony Zorr. How could she have not seen it before?

She went in search of her laptop. Settled back down on the sofa, she flipped it open and typed *Anthony Zor*r into the search engine. Only one page. No social media links. She dug through what the search engine had delivered. It led her to the front page of an Iowa newspaper.

Body of High School Girl Found at Snake River.

Kerrin pressed her fist against her mouth as she scanned the article. The pit of her stomach hardened. The girl had been Anthony's girlfriend. They'd been high school sweethearts, Homecoming King and Queen, and had planned to go to prom together.

Until she turned up dead six years ago.

Tight waves of dread spiraled through Kerrin's chest. She returned to the beginning of the article and slowed down, absorbing each word as she read.

Now she sat on the edge of her sofa, her laptop on the coffee table in front of her, elbows on her knees, kneading her hands.

I've broken a few hearts...and other things.

She did a few more searches on the internet.

The case was unsolved.

God. It was 4:00 in the afternoon. She opened a bottle of wine and plowed through the rest of the tapes. None of them made an impression. When she'd finished her third glass of wine, she texted Anthony.

Out with the girls tonight. Late. Don't bother coming over.

She tap-tap-tapped the backspace key.

Don't ever want to see you again.

Again, she tap-tap-tapped the backspace key.

Leaving town, last minute trip.

She hit the backspace key multiple times once more.

Moving out of state. Have a great life.

Jesus fucking Christ. What was she going to do?

She shuffled through Mark's notes. Thanks to the jarring image of Anthony on screen, and the even more jarring results of her internet research, she'd forgotten about them.

Anthony Zorr: Eerie quality. [In red ink] *Had to prompt for lines.*

That got actors axed in the first cut with some producers, unless you were a huge star. Which Anthony was not. If you couldn't bother to memorize your lines for the screen test, you'd likely be a drain on production.

Kerrin wondered if Frank watched the screen tests or if he would ever see Mark's notes. Unlikely.

She paced.

A dull headache clustered at the base of her skull. Maybe it was time to confess all to Norah and Joanie. She checked her messages.

Shit. Marni.

The problem was, as disturbing as Anthony's tape had been, his was the image that burned in her mind.

But she couldn't face him tonight. She couldn't face him ever again.

The thought of him touching her made her crave a power wash with industrial disinfectant.

She tried not to think about the girl whose body had been found at Snake River, or why Anthony might have killed her, as she typed: *Emergency. Don't come over. Won't be here.*

She stared at the message before pressing Send.

§§§

"What did the girl see on the third day?" Mibi asked.

"When the boy opened his mouth, she saw that he had sharp nails poking from his gums instead of teeth."

"Did he try to bite her?"

"She scooted away from him."

"But it was dark. If she scooted too far away, she wouldn't be able to see him."

"She didn't scoot that far away."

§§§

Kerrin and Joanie entered the Blue Towers lobby. It was

Tuesday night, so it wasn't too crowded. They snagged a table in the corner and exchanged idle chat until the waitress had taken their orders.

"So what's the emergency?" Joanie asked.

When they'd first been seated, Kerrin had ordered fizzy water. After drinking most of a bottle of wine that afternoon, she'd decided she didn't need any more. Now, she regretted that decision.

"What's wrong?" Joanie asked.

Kerrin told her what she could bear to confess—pretty much everything except for Anthony's drug habit, and her suspicion that he'd been the one responsible for the death of his high school girlfriend. Okay, she left out a lot.

"What am I going to do?" she asked her friend.

"Send him over to my place tonight," Joanie giggled.

"Believe me, this one you don't want."

"But you know how much I like them dark, troubled, and distant."

Kerrin was shocked to realize she had tears in her eyes. "Maybe we all do."

Joanie reached across the table to rub the back of Kerrin's hand.

"I just—"

"What Kerrin? You just what?"

"I've been so lonely."

"That's a newsflash?"

Her cheeks were wet, but Kerrin grinned. "To me."

Joanie took both her friend's hands in hers. "What you've achieved over the last fifteen years is incredible. And I know your work is fulfilling, unlike mine." Joanie was an accountant. "But, of course you've been lonely."

"God." Kerrin wiped her eyes. "Why didn't I Google him sooner?"

Joanie raised her eyebrows. They both knew the answer to that question. Having been the subject of scathing internet speculation herself, Kerrin refused to participate in the fabricated lives of the rich and famous online. "But why was I so drawn to him? How could I just let him waltz into my life and sweep me into bed?"

To her credit, Joanie just shrugged. It would have been a dangerous question for any friend to answer.

Kerrin realized she was so worked up she was almost panting.

Joanie stretched her arm across the table and grasped

Kerrin's hand. "Look, you said it yourself, you never mix business with pleasure. And when in the past fifteen years have you given yourself any time for pleasure?"

Kerrin flagged down the waitress and ordered a Black Russian. "But why him?"

"You said he's beautiful," Joanie said.

"He is. He was."

"If it's not beautiful, it doesn't cross your radar. That's why you just won the Golden Pinnacle for Best Director."

"Are you saying I'm shallow?"

"Maybe you miss some things because you're focused on aesthetics. You can't always see inner beauty on the first take."

"Thanks, Confucius."

"Don't be so hard on yourself. Maybe you're ready for a relationship, and this guy was just a way of sounding the alarm."

"I would have preferred a chiming bell to a screeching siren."

"I'm not sure you would have paid attention to a chiming bell."

Joanie pulled back her hand and brushed her fingers across her cheek bone.

Kerrin got the message. Her mascara was smeared. "Back in a minute." She grabbed her bag and headed for the ladies room.

§§§

"On the fourth day the girl saw a black outline around the boy."

Mibi sat with her legs crossed, her chin in her palms. "Like a drawing?"

"Like he was possessed by a demon."

§§§

"Mark?"

"Kerrin!"

He sat in one of the rose-colored wing chairs, intermittently shoved against the long hall between pots of enormous ficus trees, a half-glass of pink champagne in one hand, and a cigar in the other. He wore a charcoal gray suit, bow tie, and black leather boots.

"What are you doing here?" she asked.

He indicated the ladies room with his cigar. "Waiting for my sister."

The shock of running into the Assistant Casting Director

for *Demion Glass* had made her forget her mascara-streaked face, at first. Now, self-conscious, Kerrin crossed her arms. Maybe from where he sat, he couldn't see the black smudges.

"Would you like me to check on her for you?"

"That would be great," he said. "She's been in there a while. A little too much bubbly. We're celebrating the birth of my brother's first child. My parents finally have a grandchild. Takes a little bit of pressure off both of us. She got a little carried away."

"What's her name?"

"Jane."

Kerrin smiled at his parents' choice of simple, classic names.

The Blue Towers ladies room was spa-like. Stuffed sofas, gilded mirrors, blooming plants, and exotic scents filled the air. The foyer was empty. Kerrin crouched to look underneath the stalls. Second to the end, a lady kneeled, facing the porcelain god. Kerrin walked over and tapped on the door.

"Jane?"

Silence.

"Jane, Mark asked me to check on you."

The toilet flushed. The lady staggered to her feet, banging the walls of the stall. The door opened. A bleary-eyed young woman pushed past Kerrin and wobbled to the sink. She braced herself against the counter and then folded in half, dry heaving into the basin.

Kerrin walked over and rubbed her back. She was small and slim. Mark's much younger sister. The family resemblance was striking, despite her smaller nose. Although she was plain, like him, she had a quality about her that was compelling.

Kerrin rubbed her arms, uncertain how to be helpful.

The girl straightened again and turned on the faucet. "You're a lousy nurse," she said. "Could you hold up my hair while I rinse my face? I don't have anything to tie it back."

Kerrin gathered the girl's long straight hair in her hands and held it up and away from her neck.

When Jane was finished drying her hands and wiping her face with one of the monogrammed towels, she said, "Your turn."

Kerrin looked in the mirror. Her face wasn't just smudged, it looked like hair and makeup had done a bad job with war paint. Red faced, she grabbed one of the hand towels and leaned over the sink.

Hands pulled her hair way from her face and neck.

"Thank you," she said.

"Uh-huh."

Jane leaned against Kerrin when they left.

Outside, an empty-handed Mark paced. He took Jane's arm. She shifted her weight to him.

"Time to get you home," he said to his sister. "Thank you, Kerrin."

"Glad I could help."

"Yeah, she was great," Jane mumbled. "Thanks for sending her after me. I'm not sure I would have made it out alive on my own."

Kerrin appreciated the dry humor.

"You here alone?" Mark asked Kerrin.

"No." Did she imagine that flick of disappointment? "I'm with a friend—a girlfriend." Why didn't she just add—and I'm straight?

Mark smiled. "Did you get the screen tests?"

"Yes. Thank you for organizing them with such proficiency. And the notes—" She stopped herself from launching into a discussion about Anthony and the observations Mark had written in red ink. They were celebrating a birth in the family.

It wasn't the right time to discuss sinister actors. "They've been helpful. I appreciate you getting it all down."

"You're Kerrin Mayham?" Jane slurred.

"Yes."

"Congratulations on winning the Golden Pinnacle."

"Thank you."

"Have you seen my brother's screen test?" Jane asked.

Mark raised his eyebrows. He seemed a little embarrassed.

"No, did you send it along with the others?"

"I played Demion against the auditions for Elise."

The heavy weight of Anthony Zorr momentarily lifted. "I haven't gotten to those yet."

"He's better than all the rest," Jane said. "You'll see. You're going to sign him."

"You're an actor?"

"That's the dream." Mark probably wanted to muzzle his sister.

"Great," Kerrin said. "I look forward to seeing those clips."

Mark said goodnight and steered his sister toward the parking garage.

Kerrin watched his back while absorbing the memory of his face. His nose was crooked—maybe it had been broken once—

and his features were asymmetric. He wasn't unattractive, just not perfect.

"You were gone forever," Joanie said.

"I think I heard a bell chime."

Her friend shifted in her seat. "Really?"

"Maybe."

§§§

"Was the boy possessed by a demon?" Mibi asked.

"No," Kerrin said. "It was much worse than that."

Chapter 7: Frozen

As soon as Kerrin got home, she headed for her screening room and sorted through the padded envelopes for each character. When she found the Elise package, she kicked off her shoes.

Wound up after her encounter with Mark and Jane, she went to make a pot of coffee and slip into a pair of sweats. It would be impossible for her to sleep until she watched the clips.

GA-BRACK.

Her body jerked. Hot coffee burned the side of her hand.

That was her front door.

The loud bang came again. Hazy from the wine and cocktail, Kerrin tried to remember where she'd left her cell phone when she got home. She'd never had a landline installed.

GA-BRACK.

She rifled through her bag. Someone was yelling outside. She paused her frantic search to listen.

"Fucking Bitch!"

Another savage assault on the front door. Frozen in place, her brain registered the angry voice as one that was familiar to her.

Anthony Zorr.

What in the hell did he think he was doing? *Demion Glass* on reality TV?

Kerrin turned her bag upside down. Its contents careened across the counter. Lipstick and pens rolled onto the kitchen floor. A quick glance at the disarray didn't reveal her phone. She ran to her screening room. The phone wasn't visible. She jammed her hand between sofa cushions, knocking them onto the floor one-by-one. Finally, the rectangular device appeared, wedged into an indentation next to the sofa arm.

She dialed 9-1-1.

"Is this an emergency?"

"Someone is trying to break down my door."

"Are you in danger?"

"He's been at it awhile," Kerrin whispered, as if Anthony might hear her asking for help and become further enraged.

"Ma'am, you're going to have to speak up."

Kerrin pulled the phone away from her ear and thumbed speaker. "It sounds like he's using a fucking sledgehammer. If he gets through the door, safe bet, I'll be in danger."

"Thank you, ma'am."

The 9-1-1 dispatcher type-type-typed.

Kerrin crossed her eyes.

"Ma'am, are you still there?"

"Yes."

"May I have your name and address?"

"Kerrin Mayham." She gave her Hills address.

"Ma'am—"

"Yes?"

"We've received more than one call for a disturbance at that address. Units have already been dispatched. I'd like you to stay on the phone with me until the units arrive."

"Fine."

"Are you armed?" The dispatcher asked.

She had a handgun in her nightstand. "Not yet."

Sirens screamed toward her home. The crashing sounds stopped. She heard the gunning of an engine and squeal of tires before the sirens drowned everything out.

Kerrin stuck her head into the hall.

Everything was still.

"He's stopped hitting the door," she said.

"Ma'am is the intruder inside your home?"

The front door was still intact. "No, but someone's knocking on the door," Kerrin said.

"The units have arrived. The persons at your front door are police officers. Please stay on the phone with me until you make face-to-face contact with them."

"Sure."

Kerrin's heart pounded in her chest. She edged up to the peephole and identified two uniformed policemen.

When she unlocked the door, flashing red and blue lights illuminated her front yard. Kerrin ended the call with the 9-1-1 dispatcher.

"Ma'am, are you all right?" A tall and slim officer asked.

"Just scared out of my mind."

The second officer had a buzz cut. "No one was on the premises when we arrived, but we've got a unit in pursuit of a suspicious vehicle."

She hoped they had the right car.

"Were you able to get a look at the suspect?" Tall and Slim asked.

Not tonight. "No."

Several of her neighbors gathered beyond the two police cars. None of them were friends. It wasn't a friendly neighborhood. It didn't mean they weren't observant.

"Have you asked any of them?" Maybe one of them had seen Anthony tonight, or maybe one of them had seen him before tonight, coming and going from her house. It would be better for anyone besides her to identify him.

"An officer is talking with them now," Tall and Slim said.

"What about you?" Buzz Cut asked. "Do you have any ideas about who might've done this?" He stared at her, expectant.

Kerrin chewed her lower lip. If they apprehended Anthony, and she had to make a statement, she wanted Jonas to be with her. If they didn't apprehend him, and she was the first one to provide Anthony's name to the police, Marni and Colossal Talent were bound to find out. They could make her life extremely difficult by blackballing her in an industry that was tighter than a latex dress.

She shook her head. She had no idea why Anthony had attacked her door in such a rage.

But if she didn't give the police his name, and he tried again...

Kerrin rubbed her eyes.

Anthony's high school sweetheart had been bludgeoned to death. That was the only element of the crime the local police in Iowa had been certain of.

She crossed her arms. Her grip on her cell phone was so tight she feared she might crush it, but she couldn't relax her fingers. "What if you've got the wrong car? What if he tries again?" Kerrin asked.

"We'll keep a cruiser in the neighborhood. If you hear anything, call us. We'll be close by. "

"Okay."

Buzz Cut pointed to the battered exterior of the door.

Kerrin reeled. Splinters and deep grooves testified to the force of the hits. She tried not to imagine those hits aimed at her head.

"Is anyone else here with you?" Buzz Cut asked.

"No."

"Is this your home?"

"Yes."

"Do you own it?"

"Yes."

"Do you live here alone?"

He was interrogating her. "Yes."

"Do you mind if we come in and look around?"

She did. "Is that really necessary?"

Tall and Slim indicated it wasn't. Buzz Cut didn't seem pleased. The conversation shifted to more routine questions. The ones that reminded Kerrin why she'd been vulnerable to Anthony's ridiculous physical beauty in the first place. Not married. No children. No pets.

"Are you seeing anyone?"

"Nothing serious." Technically, it wasn't a lie.

"No ideas why anyone would want to beat your door down," Buzz Cut pressed.

"I'll call you if anything comes to mind," she said. "Do you have a card?"

He dug a billfold from his back pocket and handed her one.

Tall and Slim examined the door one more time. "The lock

is still intact, but I'd get someone out here tomorrow morning to replace the entire thing."

Kerrin thanked them for coming out, closed the abused door, and shut out the world. Involuntary tremors shook her entire body. They wouldn't stop. Fear, shock, and too much alcohol smashed every coherent thought except one: If he'd made it through the door, Anthony Zorr would have killed her.

She checked her phone.

No messages or texts.

Thank God, he hadn't tried to contact her.

She stared at the small dark screen, tempted to call Jonas. Her finger trembled over her phone's keypad. If she tried to speak now, she might break down.

The police had come. Anthony was gone. She was safe; no real harm had come to her. Everything was going to be all right. She could call Jonas in the morning. He could guide her through the process of getting a restraining order.

The small decision bolstered her.

Anthony wasn't Tom, and her life wasn't going to spiral completely out of control again.

In the kitchen, she switched off the coffee pot and tossed the wet grounds into the trash. Her body was calming down, but the toxic aftershocks of Anthony's insane behavior had polluted her desire to watch Mark's clips. Disappointed, she shut down her computer.

Still on edge, she walked through her house, phone in hand —flipping on every single light—checking the lock on every window—making sure all the blinds and curtains were closed. She took her handgun from the nightstand and a pillow and blanket from her bed. In the living room, she made sure her phone and gun were in easy reach, then she threw herself onto the couch and tried to get some sleep.

§§§

"Demons can be expelled," Kerrin said.

Mibi had moved. She sat on her mother's lap, her shorter legs stretched out over Kerrin's longer ones, her back rounded into her mother's belly. Kerrin twisted her daughter's hair into loose braids.

"What does expelled mean, Mommy?"

"It means a demon can be forced from the body."

"So if the boy was possessed by a demon, the girl could have made it go away?"

"Yes."

Mibi considered that. "But that's not what was wrong with

107

him, was it?"

"No."

Her daughter curled her fingers into claws. "The most beautiful boy in the world was a monster."

"And the girl couldn't believe it," Kerrin murmured. Even now, years later, recalling that night unsettled her.

"What happened on the fifth day?" Mibi asked.

§ § §

Early the next morning, laughter and loud conversation woke Kerrin up.

She tiptoed to the living room window and pushed aside just enough of the curtain to make a slit.

Four young guys wearing baggy shorts and hoodies traded bags of candy and drank from straws poked into huge takeaway soda cups. Two had cameras slung around their necks. The other two leaned against a car parked in front of her house, their rigs perched on the car's hood.

Unbelievable. Fucking paparazzi.

Kerrin's jaw set.

Who tipped them off?

Publicity boosted the bottom line of any film. Was it Frank? Or some twisted creep officed in the bowels of the studio?

Rumors of the Machiavellian lengths studios went to to make movies box office hits permeated Glitter City.

But who knew about her and Anthony? Had he bragged to someone?

Kerrin tested each suspicion against her instincts, but nothing clicked. She peeked through the window again. Damn. Now there were one-two-three-four-five-six-seven-eight of them. Their excited chatter escalated. They checked their watches and cameras.

She backed away from the window, found her phone, and retreated to her bedroom.

Maybe the answer was something simple, like the paparazzi had police scanners.

When her phone buzzed, Kerrin almost dropped it. Joanie never called this early. Anxious for safe company, Kerrin accepted the call.

"Honey, are you all right?" Joanie asked.

Kerrin hesitated. Where to begin? Better to hear why her friend had called at such an odd time. "Yeah, what's up?"

"Then you haven't seen the news yet."

"No, I fell asleep on the couch. I'm barely awake."

"The guy you told me about...wasn't his name Anthony?"

Kerrin reached for the dresser to steady herself. "Yes?"

"Honey, he died last night in a high speed car chase with the cops."

Kerrin rubbed the tight muscles in the back of her neck. "That's on the news?"

"There's more."

She closed her eyes. "What?"

"There are reports that he was an aspiring actor who'd been cast in the leading role for your next film."

Kerrin needed to throw something. She considered her phone, but she was so furious she might do it real damage. Instead, she picked up one of her gladiator sandals and slammed it against the bedroom wall. It felt so good she picked up the other one.

"What is that noise?" Joanie asked.

"Throwing shoes against the wall."

"Okay, honey, maybe you need to sit down," Joanie said.

Kerrin paced in tight circles. "I can't sit down."

"Honey, tell me when you're sitting down."

"Fine." Kerrin strode into the kitchen, pulled out a chair, and planted her butt. "Sitting."

"They're sensationalizing everything."

"Just tell me."

"Thirty-seven-year-old Kerrin Mayham, winner of the Golden Pinnacle Best Director of the Year, who's lived a hedonistic lifestyle since her affair with Tom Barnes resulted in his suicide following the breakup of his family, was a significant influence on the young Anthony Zorr. She brought him into her inner circle of friends, introduced him to drugs, and had sexual relations with him. Last night, her false accusations that he'd assaulted her led to the high speed chase that ended young Anthony's life."

Kerrin tried to breathe. She set down her phone and gasped for air. Lies. Twisted truth. She knew all too well how it was done. Fucking Marni. She'd probably sent Anthony to her house that first night. The whole thing had probably been a set up. Who knew when she'd tipped off the paparazzi? But whatever had set Anthony off last night, everything had gone off the rails. Now Colossal Talent was doing damage control. For them, spinning Kerrin Mayham into an emotionally dangerous sexual predator was a much better story than repping a psycho client who'd, in all probability, murdered his high school sweetheart.

Joanie's faint voice came from her phone. "Kerrin?"

Lightning didn't strike twice. This couldn't be happening again. "I can't talk anymore."

"I'm coming over."

"No."

"You can't be alone."

"The paparazzi already have my house staked out."

"What the hell happened?" Joanie asked.

Kerrin was too incoherent to make any sense. She ended the call and returned to the living room. The kitchen and her bedroom were too crowded with memories of Anthony. Back on the couch, she wrapped her arms around herself and rocked.

Tom's death and Anthony's death were not her fault, no matter how much the truth got twisted, she needed to hold onto reality.

§§§

"On the fifth day, the boy told the girl to stop staring at him.

"'But the witch told me to,' the girl said.

"'Do you do everything someone tells you to do?' the boy sneered.

"'When she comes back, I have to be able to answer her question. Don't you want to leave this place?'

"'No,' the boy said. The girl was baffled. All she could think about was filling her lungs with fresh air, relishing the soft heat of the sun's rays against her forehead, and sighting the full moon through a frame of towering trees."

Mibi pulled on her toes. "He's not a very nice boy."

Kerrin combed the loose braids from her daughter's hair with her fingers. "No, he isn't."

§§§

Kerrin refused to leave her home.

Norah and Joanie insisted on spending the night. The suitcases they brought along were stuffed.

When Kerrin shared her suspicion that Anthony had murdered his high school sweetheart, the revelation rendered them both speechless. The next morning, they confronted her with their decision to stay with her until she was ready to face the world again.

Kerrin was grateful.

"It will be the Longest Sleepover Ever," Joanie said.

A ghost of a smile haunted Kerrin's lips, dematerializing before it reached the corners of her mouth.

Jonas worked with Kerrin on her public statement. He also met with Frank and fielded all the studio's calls.

Kerrin could do a lot of the film prep from the house. Digital film and recording made things pretty seamless. She stopped going out with the location scout, but every night he messaged her loads of detailed files with photos. They'd worked enough sites together. He understood what she needed and provided it.

Thankfully, as the producer, Frank took everything in stride. All publicity is good publicity.

Day by day, the number of paparazzi outside her home dwindled. The neighbors complained and that helped.

Kerrin was tempted to concede casting to the Casting Director and Mark, but one morning she got up early and wanted to watch clips. This time she began with the minor characters. With the screen tests and Mark's notes, the decisions were clear-cut. She sent Mark an email.

His professional and polite response was both a relief and a disappointment. He asked when she would have input for Demion, Elise, and Sophia.

She committed to send him an email by the end of the week.

He wrote back. *Great. BTW I never got the chance to tell you how much Jane enjoyed meeting you.* Then: *Take care. Glitter*

City bites hard. Never let them chew you up and spit you out.

His simple, kind words unlocked a maelstrom of pain she'd bottled up for years. Kerrin pushed herself away from her computer, slid onto the floor and wept—honestly, deeply, and completely. She held nothing back.

The next morning she peeked out her living room window. Four guys left. Maybe the same four that had been there in the beginning. She nicknamed them The Determined Ones.

But not more determined than her.

She went to rouse Norah. "Are you up for a jog?"

"Hell to the yeah." Norah bounded out of bed like a gazelle.

Kerrin pulled her hair into a pony tail and threaded the tail through her ball cap. They went out the back door and ran down the driveway.

The catcalls escalated, flashbulbs popped around them. Kerrin stared straight ahead, her face a neutral mask. If Norah hadn't been with her, she might not have made it. When they circled back to the house after a four-mile run, the photogs were gone. They'd finally gotten what they'd come for—a payday—and then left.

Kerrin embraced the small, but important victory in

reclaiming her life.

§§§

"On the sixth day the boy picked up one of the bones and shook it in the girl's face. He gave her an awful smile with his mouthful of nails. His hair and eyes had turned pitch black.

"'You're not the first girl who's come down here to save me.'

"The beautiful boy had become so menacing, the girl's teeth chattered."

Mibi tried to make her teeth click. "I can't do it."

"It's easier when you're really cold," Kerrin said.

"Was it cold at the bottom of the stairs?"

"Yes, and everyday it was growing colder."

Mibi rubbed her arms. "Brrr."

Kerrin laughed. "And by the morning of the seventh day, when the girl woke up, her arms and legs were like icicles. She could barely move."

Chapter 8: Melting

One afternoon, Joanie was doing yoga in the living room. "Hey, Kerrin! Come here and look at this."

"What? You need me to watch you do Downward Facing Dog?"

All the windows were open. Joanie worshipped sunlight. She pointed outside. A black sedan was parked on the curb in front of Kerrin's house. A man and woman were coming up the walkway.

"They look like they should be on some cop show, don't you think?" Joanie asked.

Kerrin nodded, but waited until they knocked to go to the door. When they flashed their badges, she opened the door wide enough for them to slip inside.

Unlike Tall and Slim and Buzz Cut, these two knew who she was, the Golden Pinnacle Director of the Year. They both gushed over *A Scorched Heart*. It sounded like the woman had seen all of Kerrin's work.

After they'd paid their compliments, they asked her if she could answer a few questions about Anthony.

"Just tying up some loose ends for the paperwork," the woman said.

They wanted to discuss the night Anthony died.

Kerrin braced herself. "Is it all right if my friend joins us?"

Joanie had been a shadow in the hall. When neither the man nor the woman objected, she joined them. Everyone sat down at the kitchen table. The man pulled out a notepad.

Kerrin's jaw tightened. Maybe they weren't star struck, maybe they'd just stroked her ego to catch her off guard. She pulled her phone from her pocket and set it on the table. If things got sticky, she'd call Jonas. He'd been on speed dial since the morning after Anthony had died.

"Postmortem drug testing was performed on Mr. Zorr," the man said. "He tested positive for alcohol, marijuana, cocaine, and steroids. Did you know Mr. Zorr to be a heavy drug user?"

Kerrin took a deep breath. No one was accusing her of anything, yet. "I didn't know Anthony that well."

The man and woman exchanged glances.

"At least, not as well as I should have. I suspected his drug use, but we never discussed it. He wasn't very talkative."

"Did you see Mr. Zorr the day he died?"

For the past month, Kerrin had tried to understand how someone like Anthony had slipped under her radar.

Better to just answer the question. "Yes, he spent the night before, here. I saw him briefly that morning before he left."

"What time was that?" the man asked.

"Sometime after 8:00 am but before 10:00 am."

"Did you have any more contact with him that day, before he came and began hitting your door with an aluminum bat?"

"That's what it was?" Kerrin asked.

"Yes," the woman said.

The man repeated his question.

She didn't have to think. The text she'd sent Anthony that afternoon would be seared into her brain forever. "I sent him a text. Emergency. Don't come over. Won't be here."

"Did you, in fact, have an emergency that day, Ms. Mayham?"

"Does it matter?"

"We're just trying to establish the facts."

"No, I didn't have an emergency. I just—my whole relationship with Anthony was weird."

The man nodded, encouraging her to provide more information.

Kerrin dragged her hand through her hair. "I met Anthony and his agent, Marni Lamb, at a party at Frank Gianopoulos' home the night before the Golden Pinnacle Awards show. Frank was interested in me directing a film for his studio. We were discussing that."

God. That night seemed like it was another lifetime ago.

"He introduced me to some agents. Marni was one of them."

Kerrin's throat got dry as they quizzed her about Marni. "Does she have anything to do with this?"

Again, the pair exchanged glances.

"We recovered several items at the scene of the wreck," the woman said. "One of the items was Mr. Zorr's cell phone."

A sick feeling gathered in the pit of Kerrin's stomach.

"Did you know Mr. Zorr was having a sexual relationship with Marni Lamb at the same time he was having one with you?"

The back of Kerrin's throat burned. "Excuse me." She got up to get a glass of water and feared she would heave into the sink.

That creepy bitch.

"Are you all right?" Joanie asked, her eyes the size of saucers.

Turning her back to them, Kerrin waved her hand. "Give me a minute."

She tried not to imagine Marni Lamb, the human refrigerator, smashing the empty vase of Anthony Zorr's beauty. A strangled laugh-sob caught in her throat.

This was worse than Tom.

When she sat back down, the woman spoke. "We analyzed the text chains on Mr. Zorr's phone. I don't know how to say this—"

"Just say it," Kerrin said.

"It appears that Ms. Lamb was pimping Anthony out, not necessarily for money, but for industry favors."

The room seemed to float. She couldn't be having this conversation.

"Is it true she wanted you to push Frank Gianapoulos to hire Anthony for the lead role in the film *Demion Glass*?"

"That's true."

"When Anthony received your text that day, he passed it on to Ms. Lamb. Ms. Lamb berated him for his inability to deliver you and the favor she wanted from you. Other threats were made."

"Anthony made threats to Ms. Lamb?" Kerrin asked.

The man and woman exchanged glances, again.

"Ms. Lamb possesses incriminating evidence against Anthony Zorr for another crime," the man said.

"The murder of the girl in Iowa," Kerrin's voice was even, detached.

The woman nodded.

Joanie reached across the table and held her friend's hand.

"The girl was Marni's daughter from a first marriage. We think she found out her mother and her boyfriend were sexually involved. Perhaps she confronted him and threatened to expose their affair."

A bomb went off in Kerrin's body. Her head, her chest, her arms, her legs, everything felt disconnected. Her throat tightened as her stomach heaved. Her fingers trembled as she forced herself to remain seated. To not jump from her chair and bolt out her front door.

"We think your text, as innocuous as it was, set him off."

Kerrin chewed on her thumbnail.

"Why didn't he ever go after Ms. Lamb?" Joanie asked.

"She'd secured the evidence she had against Mr. Zorr in such a way that it would be released to the Iowa authorities upon her death."

"So he went after Kerrin instead?" Joanie asked.

"We discovered a notebook in his home," the man said. "It wasn't exactly a journal, but there were some notes and doodles. All focused on you."

Kerrin recoiled.

Obsession.

Except for those few pristine moments, when it had felt like —wordless—they'd connected.

Had Anthony genuinely been attracted to her? Had she'd been genuinely attracted to him?

Had any moment of truth existed between them? And if so,

what did that mean? That she could care for a man capable of bashing a girl's brain in? She stretched the thin fabric of her long-sleeved t-shirt to cover her wrists.

"Are you all right, Ms. Mayham?" The woman asked.

"This whole thing is just so disturbing. What were you saying?" Kerrin asked the man. She'd have plenty of time to finish the pop psychology dissection of her relationship with Anthony when they were gone.

"As I said, when Anthony passed on the information that you'd declined his services for the evening to Ms. Lamb, she berated him. He escalated his intake of drugs. We believe he came here to ascertain whether you were home, whether you had lied to him. When he discovered you were here, he became enraged. We believe that's when he returned to his car for the bat."

"You were lucky he didn't make it through the door," the woman said.

"I still don't understand why he came after me," Kerrin said.

The woman shrugged. "Maybe he thought you were lying to him, that you weren't alone."

"But I was." Kerrin shook her head. "It doesn't make sense."

"When young boys get raped by older females, the boys often convince themselves they enjoy it, that it makes them a man. It doesn't change the fact they've been violated. If they never face the truth, they become walking time bombs. Their rage at one woman becomes free floating aggression toward all women. Yet, they're always looking for a specific target to unleash that aggression on."

Joanie squeezed Kerrin's hand.

"Are you saying Marni raped Anthony when he was a boy?"

"It's just my theory," the woman said. "We don't have proof."

"Have you questioned her?" Kerrin asked.

"We did. She claims their sexual affair began after her daughter's death; that she and Anthony were comforting each other over their mutual loss, and it became something more. With her daughter and Anthony both dead, and no evidence, and no one to contradict her version of the story, we don't have grounds to hold her or charge her with statutory rape. Pandering is illegal, but it's not a high priority crime. She's out on bail."

Un-fucking-believable.

"I know it must be a lot to absorb," the woman said, "but

125

maybe knowing the facts will help you get some closure."

Kerrin didn't need closure, she needed an eraser.

The man and woman stood up.

Kerrin remained frozen in her chair. That her overwrought mind couldn't think anymore, that she felt nothing, seemed like a blessing.

They thanked her for her time.

"I'll let them out," Joanie said.

Kerrin nodded dully.

When Joanie came back to the kitchen, Kerrin still hadn't moved.

Joanie rubbed her shoulders. "Honey, are you okay?"

"I need to take a shower."

"Yeah, that's a great idea," her friend said.

Kerrin turned the water to scalding and stood under the stream until the water heater was empty.

By the time she got out, Norah was there, and her friends had cooked dinner. Kerrin wanted to retreat inside herself, but they gently coaxed her to eat with them and encouraged her to talk. It was like group therapy, but everyone focused on her.

By the time she went to bed, Kerrin felt grateful for their efforts.

Everything felt slightly less surreal.

§§§

"Did anything else happen on the seventh day?" Mibi asked.

"The girl asked the boy what had happened to the other girls who came to save him. He pointed to the pile of bones closest to him, and said, 'I ate them.'"

Mibi sat up straight. "Didn't the girl try to run away?"

"She did, but by then her fingers and toes, her arms and legs, had frozen solid."

"What about her magic shoes?"

"They froze, too."

"But wasn't her fairy godmother trying to find her? Couldn't she wave a wand and rescue her?"

"Not this time."

Mibi frowned. "What good are magic shoes and a fairy godmother if they can't save you from a witch?"

Kerrin tapped her daughter's nose. "Maybe the girl had to save herself this time."

"But she was just a girl!"

"A smart and brave girl," Kerrin reminded her.

Mibi crossed her arms.

"A small, warm place at the bottom of her heart didn't

freeze," Kerrin cajoled.

"Why not?"

"Because that was the deepest part."

Mibi rolled her eyes.

Apparently, when it came to seven-year-olds, a warm heart didn't beat magic shoes.

§§§

By the time Norah and Joanie packed up and left, life drifted toward normal.

Jonas had been a gladiator in Kerrin's defense, and two new Glitter City scandals had erupted in the month she'd lived in seclusion. It finally felt safe to get groceries and run errands.

She went to work on reorganizing, sorting, and clearing the clutter around her house. Norah would have approved. Good Feng Shui.

When she came across the black and whites of Anthony, she poured a glass of wine and settled on the sofa. Slowly, she examined each photo. Compressed into the still flat surface of a single frame, the hollowness, so apparent in his screen test, hid.

When she finished going through the stack, her impulse was to burn them. But there was someone else who might want them. She slid over to her laptop and entered *Zorr + Iowa* in the search engine. There was only one. Elizabeth. A few more searches and Kerrin had a phone number. If she waited, she knew she wouldn't call.

"Ms. Zorr?"

Kerrin introduced herself as best she could on the phone and offered her sympathies.

"I'm a photographer. I had a chance to take some black and white photos of your son. Would you like me to send them to you?"

The woman sobbed. "Oh, you're an angel. Yes, please. They would mean so much to me."

When the call ended, Kerrin's cheeks were damp. She closed her eyes and recalled the first time she'd seen Anthony, his t-shirt, jeans, flip-flops, and that bashful grin. Maybe in that single moment she'd seen who he might have been if...

If what?

If life hadn't gotten a hold of him?

If he hadn't been a raped, spoiled, entitled murderer?

She thought of her mother, Emery, fated to love troubled men who didn't love her in return. Who was Kerrin kidding?

Emery wasn't capable of love.

The question Kerrin was left with was: Was she?

§§§

"What happened when the witch came back?" Mibi asked.

"She came down the stairs with a fiery torch."

"Were the flames from the fire hot?"

"Yes, and the witch waved them close to the girl's frozen lips to melt them, so she could answer the question."

"What was the question, Mommy?"

"The witch pointed the torch toward the boy. In the halo of firelight, the boy's eyes were again a haunting blue, his hair a gleaming gold."

"'Tell me,' the witch said, 'Is he not the most beautiful boy in the world?'

"The girl blinked. The boy smiled. His teeth were pearly white. The girl felt like she was inside of a dream, and she no longer knew which part of it was real. Had she imagined the boy as a monster? If she gave the wrong answer, the witch would never let her leave, and the boy would eat her.

"Her heart bucked in her chest like a wild horse confined in a stable. She closed her eyes. 'No,' she whispered.

"'Eh? What's that? I can't hear you.'"

"The witch leaned over, and the orange wart at the end of her nose was so close to the girl's face she could have pinched it if her fingers weren't frozen."

Mibi reached up and squeezed the end of Kerrin's nose.

Her mother smiled.

"'No,' the girl answered louder and her toes melted.

"The witch frowned.

"'No,' the girl answered with more determination. She could wiggle her fingers.

"The witch glared at the girl with beady eyes.

'No, he's not the most beautiful boy in the world. You've turned him into a monster!' the girl screamed in the witch's face."

"No. No. No!" Mibi yelled.

"That's right," Kerrin encouraged her.

Her daughter stood up on the bed and shook her finger in the air. "No, he's not the most beautiful boy in the world, he's a monster."

She collapsed, giggling, in her mother's lap.

Chapter 9: The Dream of the Sad King

The next day, Kerrin was ready to face the Demion and Elise screen tests. Before settling in to watch them, she deleted Anthony's file.

Three of the actors gave promising performances, but no one delivered Demion's turn to darkness with the right edge.

After studying Mark's notes, she set the clips aside.

There were 21 screen tests for Elise. All but three were names Kerrin recognized, and four she'd directed before.

Kerrin propped her feet up on the coffee table. She pressed play.

Neither the actor nor actress wore costumes or makeup. There was no set to speak of. It was the final scene. Demion made his confession to Elise, and she forgave him, not because it was easy or natural for her to do so, but because her husband's guilt had made him psychotic, and that moved her to the core of her soul.

Kerrin understood what she wanted to see.

A demon delivered by an angel.

No melodrama. Unstripped. Honest. Real.

On screen, Mark projected an animal grace Kerrin had never noticed in person. But then again, she'd hardly seen him move. He was always seated behind some desk or in that wing chair at the Blue Towers.

His performance was nuanced, no overacting. He was generous with the actress, the way he gave her room and space to fill the screen and her lines. Not every actor was, and it was a quality that Kerrin loved, but was almost impossible to teach.

Guilt tormented me. It was my conscience—not a demon— that possessed me.

Kerrin sat up straight, her feet flat on the floor.

§ § §

"Was the girl's answer right?" Mibi asked.

"Yes. She'd seen through the witch's enchantment."

"The boy wasn't beautiful?"

"Maybe he had been at one time, but he wasn't anymore."

"That's kind of sad," Mibi said. "Did the witch let the girl go?"

"She didn't have a choice. The girl raced up the spiral staircase."

Mibi patted her hands against her thighs in a quick rhythm.

"She threw open the thick door in the oak's trunk. It slammed behind her."

Mibi clapped her hands.

"She flew past the guards and never looked back."

§ § §

Kerrin sat in her car, in the studio parking lot. She was a few minutes early for her meeting. Traffic had been light. Although her contract stipulated that she had final say on the cast, she was only going to do battle over one role.

Because of Mark's awkward position as the casting director's assistant, Kerrin wanted to present the situation to

135

Frank and to be clear about how she'd come to her decision.

This morning was going to be the first time she would see Glenda and Frank since Anthony had died. Jonas had offered to come with her. She'd been grateful, but declined. It seemed like overkill.

When Kerrin got off the elevator, Glenda stood up, came around her desk, and gave Kerrin a warm hug.

Kerrin's heart rate quickened. Tears threatened.

Glenda rubbed her back. "It's good to see you."

"Thanks," Kerrin said.

"Need anything to drink?"

"A bottle of water."

"Go on in, he's waiting for you. I'll bring the water in with his coffee." Glenda checked her watch. "It's time for his second cup of the day."

Kerrin wiped the corner of her eyes, stretched her mouth into an oversized smile, let it fall, then straightened her shoulders. She was the Golden Pinnacle Director of the Year. Frank wanted her to direct this film. He'd given her everything she'd wanted in her contract.

She could do this.

Frank was at his desk, focused on his computer screen. He

jumped up, and like Glenda, came around his titanic desk. He held out his hands to take one of Kerrin's.

"How are you holding up?"

"Better," she said.

He let go of her hand, propped his butt against his desk, and crossed his arms. "That Marni, she's a piece of work."

Kerrin let out a loud breath of agreement.

"But I have to tell you, I wouldn't have pegged her that way in a thousand years. She just seemed so square, in a let-me-don-my-apron-and-bake-some-fudge-cookies kind of way."

"Rectangular." Kerrin sketched the shape in the air with her finger. "A sinister Suzy Homemaker."

Frank tilted his head. "Definitely some hard edges."

How much of the truth did he know?

"But you didn't come here to discuss her." Frank led Kerrin toward the conference table and pulled out a chair for her. After he sat down beside her, he took out his smartphone and tapped.

Kerrin's chest relaxed. Back to business.

"So what are we talking about today? A casting issue?" he asked.

Kerrin took out the memory stick she'd loaded with all 21 of the Elise screen tests that featured Mark. She slid it toward him.

"What's this?" he asked.

"Mark Chisolm, the casting director's assistant, stood in for Demion in the Elise tests. I watched these after I'd seen all the Demion clips. He's Demion Glass. I came to you because I need you to see these."

"Have you discussed this with Mark or his boss?"

"No."

Frank picked up the memory stick and tapped it against the table top. "I've been watching your career for a long time."

Was he going to renege on giving her final say on casting?

"Thank you?" He couldn't. It was in her contract.

"Tom Barnes was a friend of mine," he said.

"I didn't realize." The words came out dry, cracked.

Was he going to tell her it was her fault? Was that why he'd hired her? So he could torment her?

Two months ago, she would never have thought such a thing, but two months ago, she could never have imagined Marni Lamb and Anthony Zorr.

"That's been the worst part of all this." Frank waved his hand in the air. "The tabloids bringing it all back up, the way he died, running after his grown kids. What a disgrace."

Kerrin gripped the arms of her chair. She wished it had an emergency button, one that could eject her to anywhere else.

"It had nothing to do with you." Frank put down the memory stick and rested his elbows on the table. "Well, not directly. Tom and I went way back, except when he was involved with you, our friendship was in a strained state. He'd been married longer than me. I'd just had my first kid with my first wife. I was still in the rosy glow of it all and being judgmental. His kids were older, he and his wife were having problems."

Kerrin didn't want to have this conversation, but her numb mind couldn't come up with any way to stop the train hurling down the tracks in her direction.

"You enchanted him," Frank said. "The first time he saw you on film, filling in for that actress—he wanted to make you a big star."

Tom had told her that.

"When everything broke, he felt awful. For his wife, for his kids, but he also felt awful for you."

Tom had tried to tell her. Unable to listen, Kerrin had cut him off. Her own guilt over the breakup of his marriage had been too heavy. She couldn't carry his too.

"But..." Frank shook his head. "Man, I'm making a mess of this. What I'm trying to say is that Tom was troubled before he met you. It wasn't your fault. If it hadn't been you, it would have been someone or something else."

Kerrin stared at her lap. She tried to take in what he'd said. For over fifteen years, she'd been waiting for someone to tell her that Tom's suicide wasn't her fault.

"Listen, life is a strange ride," he said. "You can't really explain it to someone who's fifteen or twenty-five. Hell, you barely get a grasp on it when you're my age. I saw *The Hope at the End of the World*. You were fantastic. But you're also a great director. One of the best."

Kerrin raised her chin and gazed at Frank.

"Look," he said. "I'm not saying any of that was easy for you. What I am saying is: What you did with it, the choices you made, drilling down into your talent, creating something of real value, instead of letting it destroy you. That's what life is really about."

"Thank you." She barely heard the words herself.

He gave his head that tilt she was becoming familiar with.

"Ah, I'm crap at this. All you need to know is that me and the studio are behind you 100%."

"Thank you. That's good to know."

He slapped the table. "So you want Mark Chisolm for Demion Glass?"

"I do."

Frank slipped the memory stick into his shirt pocket. "I'll watch these. He's done some small parts for us before. I like him," he said.

The storm had passed.

Kerrin felt like she'd swallowed a rainbow.

§§§

"What happened to the girl after she escaped from the witch and the monster boy?"

"She wandered in the woods."

"All alone?" Mibi asked.

"For a little while."

"Was she lonely?"

"A little bit, until one night she had a dream."

"What was it about?"

"The sad king."

Mibi wiggled down in Kerrin's lap. The length of her body

pressed against her mother's legs, her head rested in her mother's lap. She reached up and held her mother's cheeks, so Kerrin had to gaze into her eyes. "Why was the king so sad?"

"Who knows? So many sad things happen in life."

Mibi fell quiet, tapping her fingertips against her mother's jawbone.

"But that night," Kerrin made her voice cheerful, "in the girl's dream, he'd stopped crying, and the sun was out, shining."

"Was the world still drowning in water?"

"No, the earth had soaked up the sad king's tears, and flowers had begun to bloom. The entire world was covered with flowers in every imaginable color, even the deserts."

"Did the dream make the girl happier?"

"It did."

Mibi dropped her hands and closed her eyes.

§§§

Kerrin stepped out of the elevator. She waved to the people she passed on the way to Mark's cubicle.

He was on the phone. When he saw her, his face lit up.

Kerrin returned the smile. She felt giddy. His wrinkled button-down shirt, faded jeans, and loafers without socks looked good on him.

He motioned to an empty chair at the table that filled his cubicle. Kerrin had too much energy to sit. She waved him off.

Mark stood up. "Great, thanks. Yeah, next week." He slid his cell phone into his pocket and held out his hand.

Kerrin shook it. His fingers felt gently warm against her palm.

"To what do I owe the pleasure?" he asked.

His unabashed delight with her unexpected visit gave her confidence to go forward with her impulse.

"Have you eaten lunch yet?" she asked.

"No." He rubbed his stomach. "But, man, am I hungry!"

"Want to join me at Caesar's?"

His eyes flickered.

"Not a salad guy?"

"Salad's great. What's the occasion?"

Kerrin shrugged. "It's a beautiful day?"

He bobbed his chin. "I can go with that."

She leaned in and said, "I appreciated your emails."

He rubbed his jaw. "I hated to see you go through that."

"That makes two of us."

He stopped by the fourth floor receptionist to let her know

he was stepping out for lunch.

Outside, he said, "I'll drive."

"Sure."

He led her to a beat up truck.

Kerrin's heart danced. She respected anyone who made sacrifices to achieve their dreams. When he held open the door for her, she thanked him with a wide grin.

He had to park a few blocks away from the restaurant. While they walked side by side, he filled her in on how the cast was shaping up.

Hyper-aware of his proximity, Kerrin listened.

At the restaurant, she ordered her standby salmon Caesar. He ordered the grilled ribeye Caesar. Kerrin asked after Jane.

"She's doing great."

"Yeah?"

"She's a costume designer and just got her first theater gig."

"That's wonderful," Kerrin said.

"She's already throwing herself into it with everything's she's got."

"You two have always been close?"

"I'm the oldest boy, she's the youngest girl. I've always looked out for her."

His ringtone, a wailing electric guitar, went off. He actually blushed as he checked it. "I need to take this," he said. "Frank," he mouthed.

A wave of bright light swelled in Kerrin's chest.

"Yes, sir. Yes." He checked the time on his phone. "I'll be there at 2:00."

He didn't look at her when he slipped his phone back into his pocket. He stared briefly at his salad before looking up. "We've been waiting on your input to cast Elise. Have you looked at the clips?"

"I did."

He nodded.

"Several of the actresses were really good," she said, drawing out her own excited anticipation to his response to Frank's news. "It was tough to make a final call. Your notes helped."

"Great." Speckles of light infused his warm brown eyes.

She took a careful sip of water, aware of the delight playing at the edge of her lips.

"And Demion?"

Kerrin couldn't stop smiling. It made it difficult to answer him.

He quirked an eyebrow.

"You know it's a great part—a career-making part. And I struggled, so many talented auditions."

He crossed his arms and rested his elbows on the table.

"But—Jane was right."

Before she registered what was happening, he'd pushed his chair back, gotten up from the table, and was holding out his arms.

Uncertain how to interpret the spontaneous gesture, she froze. If she didn't stand up soon, he'd look like an idiot. She clenched her napkin to keep from throwing herself at him as she rose from her seat.

His arms were strong around her.

"Thank you," he said.

Kerrin resisted leaning into his chest. Any struggling actor would be overjoyed at getting the part.

§§§

Kerrin shifted. She rolled her daughter off her lap and pulled the sheet and blanket up to her chin. She reached to turn off the lamp.

Mibi's hand caught her forearm. "Did the girl stop looking for beauty?"

Kerrin leaned over her daughter and hugged her tight.

"No," she whispered. "She never stopped looking for beauty, but the girl's experience with the witch and the monster boy had made her wiser."

"I'm glad," Mibi said. "Is that the end of the story?"

Kerrin let her daughter go and sat up. "There's a little bit more."

Mibi struggled to keep her eyes open. "Tell me."

Chapter 10: The Shepherd Boy

Six months later, Kerrin, Norah, and Joanie sipped champagne martinis in the Blue Towers lobby bar.

"We're waiting," Joanie said.

"No holding back," Norah added.

Kerrin caressed the stem of her glass. After *Demion Glass* had wrapped in the wee hours of the morning, she'd gone home and crashed for fifteen solid hours. The official wrap party was Friday night, but Norah and Joanie had insisted on their traditional in-the-can celebration tonight.

They wanted to hear all about Mark.

Kerrin smiled. "He's—" She struggled to find the right words.

"He's what?" Norah asked.

"Have you two hit the sheets?" Joanie asked. "That's all I need to know."

"No." Not for lack of desire on her part. Some nights, after long days of intense interaction, she'd fallen into bed, hugging her pillow with her entire body. "He's hard to read, the consummate professional."

"It's his eyebrows." After he'd officially been cast as Demion, Norah had studied Mark's head shot. "They're almost straight. It means he has an even temperament."

Joanie slumped. "Does that mean he's not passionate?"

"It means he's not going to show up on Kerrin's doorstep with a baseball bat," Norah said.

They fell quiet.

"For starters," Kerrin said. "My gut tells me this is the best work I've ever done."

Norah shrugged her shoulders at Joanie. "That's great, right?"

"Yeah, because everything else you've ever done is such a piece of crap," Joanie said.

Kerrin traced the rim of her glass with her finger. "Over the years, my crew has learned to work with me, and I've always had a clear vision of what I want to see in each scene, but sometimes in the past, I've been impatient. Grumpy." She smiled. "My rough edges aren't as sharp when Mark's nearby."

"Then he's like a teddy bear or something?" Joanie picked out the cashews from the bowl of nuts. "Love to cuddle."

Kerrin laughed. "That's not what I meant."

Joanie raised her eyebrows and her hands.

"Whenever he's not around, I can feel it," Kerrin said. "I miss him."

"You like him a lot," Norah said.

"I don't get it," Joanie said. "You like him—like a good friend? Is he seeing someone else?"

"He never talks about anyone else, and the only person who ever visited him on set was his sister, Jane." Kerrin gulped her martini. "He's great with her. He's great with everyone. And my God, he was so good as Demion. Every single scene, every single shot. I don't know how he did it."

"You have a crush on him," Joanie said. "A big one."

"But does he have feelings for me?" Kerrin asked. "Besides professional respect? And gratitude for helping him get the part?" Her phone on the marble counter in front of her chimed.

"Was that a *chime*?" Joanie grabbed the phone before Kerrin could pick it up. "Someone wants to go to dinner!"

Kerrin held out her hand. Her friend begrudgingly relinquished the phone. Kerrin peered at the screen, breathless.

Dinner? Soon.

"It's Mark," Joanie narrated to Norah.

"Maybe he wants to express his professional respect," Norah teased.

Kerrin ignored them, but it was impossible to ignore the wild hope bucking in her chest. *Sure*, she texted.

Thursday night?

What time?

Pick you up at 8:00?

Look forward to it.

See you then.

Kerrin gave her phone back to Joanie. Her friends hunched over the small screen.

"We're having brunch on Sunday," Joanie said. "And I

expect the quality of your confessions to be way upped."

§ § §

"One day the girl cut through a pasture where a shepherd watched over a flock of sheep."

"Was he beautiful?"

Kerrin scratched her neck. "He wasn't ugly, but his face was long, and his hair was a frightful mess. He wore scratchy, dull-colored clothes, and he smelled like dirt, but he was friendly, and he offered to share his lunch of bread and cheese with her."

Mibi closed her eyes again.

§ § §

Kerrin watched Mark finish his Boti Kebab. When he'd suggested Amaya's, she'd been curious. More of a dive than most restaurants she frequented, it had a reputation for fresh, well-prepared dishes. Maybe she should eat Indian food more often. The Prawn Tikka had been delicious.

When the waitress came to clear their dishes, Mark ordered a pot of chai tea. He watched the young woman leave before he returned Kerrin's gaze.

The lights in the restaurant were dim, and their booth was cozy. They'd already made small talk, discussed the food, the end of filming, and his sister.

"Working with you has been a great opportunity," he said.

Kerrin fiddled with her napkin. This dinner was about Mark expressing his professional respect. All night she'd been relaxed and light hearted. Now, she slipped back into professional mode as she tried to hide her disappointment. "I can say the same. You made my job both easy and challenging."

"Challenging, how so?"

Kerrin forced her voice to remain light. She'd so hoped he'd reciprocated her feelings. "I always know what I want to see before I start shooting. But you'd do something—maybe it was the way you interpreted the subtext for a line or the blocking. It would make me imagine something different, and that was exciting." Most actors who gave her another vision annoyed her.

"Thank you," he said. He crossed his arms and rested his elbows on the table, that familiar but friendly stance.

Embarrassed by how she'd misread the evening, Kerrin avoided meeting his gaze.

The tea came. She welcomed the diversion.

He filled her cup first. Always the gentleman. So easy to

attribute meaning where there was none. She'd made his career. He was grateful. That was all.

He offered her milk and sugar. The aromatic tea was delicious. If she indulged another cup, she would be up all night. Alone.

Kerrin's thoughts darted as she rushed to rearrange her hopes for the future. Maybe she needed to get a pet. A dog. A big one like Boomer.

Across from her, Mark settled back into the booth. "As great as working with you has been–"

Was he blushing?

"I have to tell you," he said, "I'm very attracted to you."

Kerrin choked. It felt like her face was turning purple. Mark made it half-way up from his seat before she waved him down. Gasping for breath, she wiped her eyes with her napkin.

"Are you all right?" he asked.

"Tea," the word came out a strangled utterance. She took a sip of water. "It went down the wrong way. I'm fine." She took a few more drinks of water to make sure the next time she opened her mouth she didn't sound like a frog.

He waited while she collected herself. "I'll admit that wasn't quite the reaction I was hoping for," he said.

Her mind still wasn't working. "It wasn't you." Kerrin pointed to the pot. "I'm sorry, what did you say?"

"As much as I value our professional relationship, and working with you has been amazing, I'd rather date you," he said.

It felt like the sun had relocated in her belly. "I...you? Okay."

"Is that 'okay, you heard what I said,' or 'okay, you'd like to date me, too'?"

This was it. It was happening. Right now. She hadn't just imagined it. He was attracted to her! Her heartbeat seemed to rise into her throat. It made it hard to speak! Kerrin let her hand fall onto his.

He was waiting for her response.

Finally, some words came. "I'd like to date you too."

He turned his hand over to hold hers. The warmth of his palm and fingers drew her attention. The entire restaurant and everyone in it was reduced to the single point where their skin touched. When she looked up, he gazed directly into her eyes. It flustered her. She brushed a stray hair from her face with her free hand. A flip comment dissolved on her tongue.

He reached for her other hand.

Her heart pounded like a kettle drum.

"Where do we go from here?" she asked.

"If I take you home, I might not ever be able to let you leave," he said.

"What if I promise I'll always come back?"

"I could live with that." He pushed the empty tea pot and cups and saucers out of the way and leaned his entire torso across the table. When his lips found hers, the melting surrender wasn't just sexy, it was like she'd reached harbor.

§§§

Kerrin lowered her voice. "When the sun began to set, the shepherd boy asked the girl where she lived. When she told him she lived alone, he invited her to come home with him. She could live with his family. He had a sister named Jane. They could all be friends."

Mibi's eyes flew open. "My aunt's name is Jane."

"Yes, it is."

"Was the boy's name Mark?"

"How did you know?"

"Did they live happily ever after?"

§§§

Friday morning when Kerrin got home, she went straight to

her closet and pulled out her grandmother's rhinestone pumps. She slipped off her ankle boots and slid her foot into one pump then the other. Humming, she crossed her bedroom to her dresser and rummaged through the bottom drawer—her memorabilia drawer. When her fingers brushed the hard perimeter of the costume crown Hannah had bought for her all those years ago, she pulled it out of the drawer.

Its fake gemstones—a few were missing—winked in the rays of light filtering through the blinds. Kerrin walked into the hall and stood in front of the long mirror. She positioned the old keepsake on her head.

Hannah's voice whispered through the years, You're a fairy princess. All of your dreams will come true.

Kerrin spun herself and stopped. With the heel of one pump in the air, she struck the regal pose that used to make her and her grandmother burst into laughter.

"As long as you believe," Kerrin whispered.

The woman who looked back from the mirror was a happy one.

She went into the kitchen to make a sandwich, and when she settled on the sofa to eat it, the crown was still on her head. She left it there as she kicked off the pumps, slid back into her sofa, and pressed play.

Mark entered the screen.

He and life were beautiful–beautiful.

§§§

Kerrin kissed her daughter's forehead.

Mirabella always fell asleep before she got to the part where the shepherd boy transformed into the most beautiful boy in the world.

Mark stuck his head into his daughter's room.

Kerrin mouthed, "She's asleep," and turned off the lamp.

She tiptoed to the door. When she reached him, Mark enfolded her in his arms. Kerrin softened into him.

They lingered in that timeless space, absorbing each other's presence. When her entire body had relaxed, he took her hand and led her toward their bedroom.

Telling Mirabella *beauty beauty* always made the miracle of Kerrin's relationship with Mark tangible.

"What are you smiling about?" he asked.

"Me and you."

"You never thought we'd last," he said.

"It is all your fault."

"What?"

"Before I met you, I didn't believe in happily ever afters. Not deep in my heart, you know? I thought they made for great scripts, but I never believed I'd get one of my own."

"Are you saying I'm your Prince Charming?"

"Absolutely."

"Lucky me," he said.

He still amazed her. Every day he remained the same wonderful man. No dark, hidden secrets. No pathological artistic angst. No inexplicable emotional withdrawal. Sometimes it was still hard to wrap her head around how beautiful their life together was.

"No, lucky me." And she knew it.

She'd weathered bleak winter and life had brought her Mark and Mirabella, her tulips, blossoming on the first day of spring.

Author's Note

I chose Han's Christian Andersen's "Beautiful" also titled "Beauty of Form and Mind" for the first retelling in my *Once Upon a Time Today* collection because beauty is something that has always moved and fascinated me, it's one of my obsessions. I do believe that whether one wishes to acknowledge it or not, beauty has a lot of power. However, the question of what is beautiful is very personal. And though our perceptions of beauty are influenced by our families and culture, we all ultimately perceive the beautiful distinctly.

In Andersen's tale, a male sculptor is besotted with a

beautiful but quiet young lady. He misinterprets her reticence as depth and proceeds to marry her. As he lives with her, he discovers his wife's lack of speech isn't so much that "still waters run deep", more that she's rather passive and insipid. His awareness of her nature comes too late. It doesn't help that the young lady's overbearing mother moves in with the newlyweds.

Suffice it to say that by the end of the tale, the sculptor's eye for beauty has altered and matured.

To make this tale contemporary, I chose a female protagonist, Kerrin Mayham. She needed to be driven by beauty, so a film director seemed like the perfect profession. I wanted to remain true to the protagonist misjudging the interior of someone who was physically beautiful. Enter aspiring actor Anthony Zorr.

While he doesn't have an overbearing mother, he does have an aggressive agent in Marni Lamb. The story unfolds from there.

I added the narrative frame because I wanted to add another layer of enchantment to the tale. Allowing Kerrin to create a fairy tale by drawing from the experiences in her life, allowed me to recreate one of the special memories I shared with my own mother who seemed to spin the most fantastical tales out of nothing when I was child. Who knows? Perhaps she was drawing from the well of her experience too.

Thank You

I appreciate you spending your valuable time reading *Beautiful Beautiful*. If you'd like to share the story with other readers, please tell a friend, or post a review on any book-ish site.

I'd also like to invite you to sign up for my newsletter: http://eepurl.com/wWKUj. It's quirky–like me:D–and I confess, it comes out sporadically, but I send a variety of things, including some (hopefully) pleasant surprises along with updates on all my new releases.

Sincerely,

First Chapter of Dreaming of the Sea

2005 –

Nine-year-old Miriam clutched her pink sock monkey as she stared at the television. Perched on the edge of the sofa, because she could never properly balance in the enormous and uncomfortable dip in its middle, she ran her tongue over the ridges of her chapped lower lip. When she found a bit of loose skin she chewed it off. It was impossible to concentrate on what Ernie and the Cookie Monster were saying. The escalating grunts and murmurs coming from the apartment's single bedroom split her attention, even though the door was closed.

It was winter, and the apartment was cold. As the sun set, the temperature inside became frigid. Miriam's oversized sweats and thin t-shirt offered little warmth as the living room darkened. Her mother often turned off the heat to save money. Miriam rubbed her eyes. The two hours of Sesame Street reruns were almost finished. Her favorite show, My Little Pony, was next. Her stomach gurgled. She glanced at the closed bedroom door and strained her ears. They must be passed out. If she was lucky they'd remain that way until morning, and Miriam would be at school when the bedroom door finally opened.

Sometimes she got lucky.

The kitchen and living room were one space, separated by a counter. On the way to the pantry, Miriam carefully stepped around the squeaky spot beneath the stained carpet. Besides the ends of a loaf of bread in a knotted plastic sack, there wasn't much on the shelves. Jars of peanut butter, mustard, pickle relish, and a few cans of Campbell soup. A bowl of soup would warm her up, but she couldn't risk banging the pot against the stove. A peanut butter and jelly sandwich would have to do.

Miriam reached for the bread and peanut butter. She set them down softly on the kitchen counter. She stood before the refrigerator and sucked in her breath. If she wasn't careful, the door would make a loud smack when it closed. Maybe she should forget the jelly.

She glanced back at the bedroom door. It remained safely closed. A peanut butter and jelly sandwich would taste so good. Miriam yanked on the refrigerator door. Light spilled out. It was as empty as the pantry, but there was a half-full jar of grape jelly on the side door. She eased it out. With her other hand, she gripped the door handle. When it was almost closed, she let go. It made a slight pop as it sealed. Miriam froze.

Her pulse pounded in her ears as she slowly turned. Miriam screamed and dropped the jar. It rolled across the floor until it banged against the bottom of the refrigerator.

The man her mother had brought home earlier leaned with his elbows against the counter, watching her. His long stringy hair reached past his shoulders. Miriam couldn't begin to count the number of tattoos on the threatening bare skin of his arms and chest.

She backed away as he came around the counter and picked up the jelly.

He pulled open the refrigerator and slid the jar next to a six-pack of beer. He crouched down in front of Miriam, who stood with her back against the wall. "You can have dinner after we play."

Miriam's stomach heaved. He took her hand. She refused to walk. He pulled harder. Her sock-covered feet slid.

"She doesn't want to come," he shouted to Miriam's mother.

Lights flicked on in the bedroom.

Once attractive, Helen now looked used up. Gaunt and sallow, a belt circled her bicep. She staggered toward the man and her daughter. "Hey, honey, don't you want to play fashion model?"

Miriam's eyes welled with tears. Fashion models wore clothes.

§§§

The 1500s –

Once upon a time, a woman tempted to throw herself from a seaside cliff onto the killing rocks below paused to reconsider: Would it be more satisfying if her lover could feel the agony that ripped her heart to shreds and pulverized its remaining tissue with meaty blows? Yes, she thought. Revenge would be more sweet than immolation.

Her plea, so genuine and determined, reached the devil's ear. It was just the kind of dilemma he relished.

When he arrived on the blustery promontory, he paid his compliments. "In the throes of devastating betrayal, few have the presence of mind to stop and think. Yet how much more satisfying than suicide is an eye for an eye—a tooth for a tooth—a heart for a heart."

The woman seethed. She dug her fingernails into her palms, drawing blood. The devil caught a whiff. He encouraged her to confide her tale.

"The man I believed mine—" The woman banged her wounded hand against her breast. Two drops of blood speckled the front of her simple dress. She broke down, hiccoughing, before she wiped her tears away, leaving a smear of blood from her cheek to her chin. "He's a sailor. His easy lies concealed wives, lovers, and children. He abandons them in every port like stray dogs. I found proof in a wooden chest he keeps locked away in his boat. Oh, he denied it all, until I shoved those love letters and trinkets down his throat." She laughed, it was a gash to the ears. "After he choked them up, he gloated over my naiveté. 'Did you think you were the only one?'" The woman moaned.

"I know of a volcano," the devil said, for he'd contrived an elegant solution.

The woman listened with every pore.

"It's at the bottom of the sea and needs tending."

"What kind of care does a volcano require, especially one on the ocean floor?"

"It would be better if it had some kind of guardian," the devil's tone was matter-of-fact; it always was when ploughing the ground for the purchase of a soul. "A witch is what I'm thinking," he said.

"What kind of a witch?"

"A sea witch."

"And how will that suit my need for revenge?"

"Oh, it will suit your need very well. I'll grant you the ability to draw from the volcano's raw power. In its proximity, you'll control the very sea. And it's not far from here." The devil pointed to the cove. "Your man, does he sail these waters with some frequency?" He drew a square in the air between the visible shore and the sea's horizon.

"Yes, his routes are most commonly in these waters."

"Then you might conjure a sea storm, and when his wrecked ship sinks to the ocean floor, you could salvage his bones. Make some little knickknacks with them."

"Where would I keep them?"

The devil stroked his goatee, for he'd chosen an urbane facade. "You would need a lair, I think. A place of your own, in the volcano's shadow."

"But I can't live underwater!"

"Ah." The devil clasped his hands behind his back. The movement pulled open his grey tweed jacket and exposed his fine white shirt, satin vest, and the gold chain of a pocket watch. He liked to attend to details when he made these appearances. "I've forgotten to mention the best part haven't I?" The woman's puzzled expression encouraged him. She would agree to the pact, he was certain. "There are creatures who inhabit the sea—light-filled vermin who sing and celebrate all the time. They're rather annoying in their banality." He sniffed. "Perhaps you've heard of them. They're called mermaids."

"Oh, they're nothing but storybook creatures—they're not real."

"I assure you they are." The devil put his hands in his pockets and made a half-turn. "Walk with me."

She followed along beside him.

"Let's say, you're not only the volcano's custodian, but you're also given the power to take and restore the ability to live in the sea." He paused his stride. "You could take a mermaid's fins and replace them with legs. Or you could take a mortal's legs and replace them with fins." He released his chin and waved a hand in the air. "Of course, you'd have the talent for the usual spells and draughts too. "

The woman held up her hand and ticked off the devil's promises. "Keeper of the volcano, ability to create sea storms, giver and taker of fins and legs, talent for spells and draughts, plus my own little cottage on the ocean floor."

"Yes, yes, of course."

It all sounded to good to be true. "You'll be wanting something from me, I suppose."

"Only your soul."

The woman wasn't the god-fearing type; she wasn't even convinced she had a soul. "That's all, my soul?"

"With the many powers I'm bestowing upon you, and given the blackness roiling in your heart, I imagine you'll be up to all sorts of no good. You don't want to have to pay for all that in the afterlife, do you?"

The woman snorted. "Of course not."

"Didn't think so. The day you die, I'll harvest your soul and leave you to slumber peacefully through eternity."

The woman liked to sleep. "And if you don't take my soul? What will happen to me then?"

"That will depend on the the quality of your choices while you're alive."

"Then it's true, all that stuff about heaven and hell," the woman murmured. Being no saint, she hated to think of the crimes she might already be spiritually indebted for.

"Very true."

"Maybe it's better if I don't–"

"Have to take responsibility for any of your actions."

"Exactly." She considered his proposition a bit more and realized she'd come out on top. "I don't know why more folks don't deal directly with you."

"It's a mystery to me as well." The devil chuckled. "There is one more small matter."

The woman's fantasies of extracting vengeance from her lover came to a halt. What more could there be?

"It would be splendid if you could locate an apprentice who'll take your place before you die," the devil said. "In fact, I think I'll make that part of the contract."

The woman plucked at her dress. "But how will I find one?"

The devil gave her question some thought. "I see your point. It would be hard, if not impossible, to convince one of those simpering mermaids to take your place. Perhaps you should be amphibious," he mused.

"What does that mean?"

"You'll be able to walk on land and swim in the sea. You'll be the only one who can."

"You mean I'll have legs when I'm not in the water?"

"Yes, and fins when you're in the sea. Rather ingenious, don't you think? It will make it much easier to find a mortal to serve as your apprentice."

"Oh, all right. I suppose that's not too much to ask."

"I thought not."

And so, the first sea witch in a long line of sea witches came into being.

§§§

1852 –

Nine-year-old Gertrude lazed on a pile of rubble outside the sea witch's lair. The stack of rotting clothes, disintegrating maps, and swathes of decomposing canvas, which had once waved in sea breezes and snapped in crosswinds as proud sails, overflowed a warped crate re-shaped to Gertrude's body. The make-shift couch was the sea witch's apprentice preferred spot to kill time.

In the depths of her lair, Beulah, gulped and sputtered. The sea witch was a noisy sleeper. At least she wasn't nagging Gertrude to collect fecal pellets, fungi, sea urchin spines, or worms this afternoon. Gertrude chewed on a thumbnail. No matter how assiduously she gnawed the thick, gray thing, it never broke or splintered. In her peripheral vision, the snake-like coils of her hair writhed as if they were alive. She did her best to ignore them as she passed some gas. As usual, she'd eaten too much mush.

Beulah boiled water spiders, water snakes, and water bugs over kettles of lava extracted from the nearby volcano. The tasty stew was the only thing about being the sea witch's apprentice that Gertrude liked, and she always ate too much of it.

She shifted on the mound of trash as another puff of wind escaped her blob-shaped body. Her gaze followed the yellow-green cloud until it collided with a glimmer of light. What's this? Gertrude pushed herself up onto her wrists.

The glow swam in her direction. It haloed a creature unlike any Gertrude had ever seen. Her eyes widened at the sight of the silky golden hair, creamy complexion, and graceful tail fin covered in a mosaic of shimmering scales.

"Are you the sea witch?" the creature trilled.

Gertrude gaped and shook her head.

"Do you know where she lives?"

Gertrude pointed to the dark opening behind her. "What are you?" she asked the creature in her rough voice.

"A mermaid."

"I'll tell Beulah you're here."

"Thank you." The mermaid twirled her slim hands in graceful spirals, treading water.

"Beulah!" Gertrude yelled. Her eyes remained on the mermaid's pearly fingernails.

"What are you yapping about now?" Beulah grumbled from the lair's interior.

"Are you here for a spell?" Gertrude tried to soften her voice, but it came out more like a hiss.

The mermaid arched backward as she nodded.

"Customer!" Gertrude yelled. "Go on inside."

The mermaid hesitated before swishing her sparkly tail to propel her into the depths of the sea witch's lair.

Inside, Beulah sat on her own throne of trash. "Well, what do you want?"

"I need legs—human ones. I've been told you have the power to—" The mermaid's graceful tail went limp under the gaze of Beulah's beady eyes. "Grant my wish."

"I don't grant anything." Beulah ran her finger over a pile of bottles filled with rays of fluorescent gold, blue, green, and pink. "My potions and spells are costly."

Gertrude thought the mermaid's eyes watered. Although, at the bottom of the sea, it was always hard to tell.

"I don't have any gold."

"No? That's too bad."

"I must have a pair of human legs." The mermaid's hands fluttered to her chest. "I've fallen in love."

"Of course you have," Beulah snickered. "Do you have anything of value?"

The mermaid blinked her blue eyes. "Why, I don't know."

Beulah grunted. "If you can't pay for the potion, you won't be getting any legs."

Gertrude watched the exchange with increasing interest. "Do you have any jewelry?"

The mermaid gave her head a sorrowful shake.

"Maybe you know where a treasure chest is buried?" Gertrude prompted, although she wasn't exactly sure why she wanted to help the mermaid.

"No," the mermaid whispered.

"Then go on. Get of here." Beulah waved her lumpy arms.

"I can sing," the mermaid said. "I've been told I have a beautiful voice."

Beulah's brow creased. "Let me hear a song."

The mermaid closed her eyes and clasped her hands. Even though her sweet-sounding voice quavered and trembled, it was a delicate and alluring sound.

When she was finished singing, Beulah's eyes narrowed. "I'll trade your voice for a pair of legs."

The mermaid agreed.

"You understand you won't ever be able to speak again, and every time you take a step on those human legs it's going to feel like you're walking on a pair of knives."

Gertrude thought the mermaid's eyes were tearing up again, even as she clung to the bargain.

"All trades are final. There's no taking it back if your human doesn't return your love."

The mermaid fluttered her eyelashes. "I understand."

"Well, then."

Gertrude hovered nearby as the sea witch boiled some worms and crab eyes.

Beulah tossed two handfuls of smashed snail shells into the pot as she muttered an incantation. At the last minute the sea witch whipped out her free hand to catch a handful of her apprentice's skirt. "Bring me the yellow one and the blue one." The sea witch pointed to the coral-colored vials on the shelf of bones.

Gertrude obeyed.

Beulah stirred all of the yellow elixir and half of the blue into the pot before refilling each vial with the bubbling ingredients. Now, the liquid in the first vial was a muddy brown and the liquid in the second was a deep, slimy green. Beulah gave the muddy brown potion to the mermaid. "It will scrape your throat going down, but when it comes back up it will bring your voice with it."

The mermaid's pale skin turned paler.

"Get the bucket," Beulah ordered Gertrude. When her

apprentice had the rusted pail in hand, the sea witch told the mermaid to drink up.

She did.

"Every last drop," Beulah croaked.

The drained vial slipped from the mermaid's fingers. Her lips pursed, her eyes rolled, she clutched her throat, her entire body convulsed.

Gertrude couldn't believe anyone would willingly undergo such treatment for anything.

When the mermaid began to choke, Beulah shoved the swamp green vial at Gertrude at the same time she grabbed the bucket from her. "Don't just stand there like an idiot. You have to catch her voice!"

A radiant spittle erupted from the mermaid's small mouth.

Beulah captured every drop. Her black eyes shined with glee.

When the mermaid opened her mouth, she winced. No sound came out.

"Your throat is raw. It will heal in time. But you'll never speak or sing again." Beulah cackled.

For the first time Gertrude truly contemplated the power that would someday be hers.

Beulah told her apprentice to give the mermaid the second potion. "Don't take it until you're on land. Otherwise you might drown." The sea witch cackled again. "It's going to feel like someone is sawing off your tail fin and nailing legs in its place. But maybe your human will return your love, and it will all be worth it."

The mermaid's eyes remained downcast as she draped the vial's chain around her neck then hurriedly exited the lair.

Gertrude was full of questions. "Why are we so ugly?"

"Witches must be fierce creatures." The sea witch nodded toward the retreating mermaid. "Who would be afraid of her?"

"Maybe fear isn't the only kind of power. Did you see how even the eels stopped to look at her?"

Beulah whacked Gertrude on the side of the head. "Be grateful for what you've got." The sea witch smashed a handful of poached sea beetles into her mouth. "There's lots of girls who'd be glad to take your place. Your mother did you a favor by bringing you to me early on. You've got lots of time to study and develop your cunning. By the time I'm gone, you'll be one of the most powerful sea witches who ever lived."

Gertrude never liked to be reminded of her mother who'd traded her to the sea witch for a love potion when Gertrude was still an infant. "It would be easier to understand why the mermaid wanted to trade her tail fin if she had a black snake tail like you and me."

Beulah cuffed her again. "Nothing is wrong with our tails, girl."

The back of Gertrude's head smarted.

"If you ask me, that mermaid is stupid," Beulah squawked.

"What are you going to do with her voice?"

"Hoard it." Beulah gave Gertrude's ear a painful tweak. "I don't like to let go of anything. You never know when it might come in handy."

"Have you ever been on land?" Gertrude asked her mentor.

"Last time I went up there, I got you. I don't want for anything else. Taking trips is a waste of time if you ask me. Home sweet home is my motto."

Gertrude fell silent. Beulah, often exhausted after working magic, spread out on a trough of bones.

When the sea witch began to snore, her apprentice swam after the mermaid. Hiding in the shadows, Gertrude tried to catch up with the mesmerizing creature.

By the time Gertrude reached the border of their waters, the mermaid's light had receded to a faint flicker overhead.

Gertrude watched the slim ray of light as it continued to ascend. After it disappeared, she began to wonder: If her hair was smooth and flowing, not snake-like; if her complexion was fair, not pocked and scarred; if her form was comely, not in the shape of a blob with crooked hands and teeth protruding, would she be more powerful than Beulah?

It set Gertrude to dreaming.

About the Author

Heidi Garrett is the author of the *Daughter of Light* fantasy trilogy about a young half-faerie, half-mortal searching for her place in the Whole.

She's also the author of *Once Upon a Time Today*, a collection of modern fairy tale retellings for adults who have already left home. *The Magic Cupcake* series is paranormal romance trilogy she writes with Billie Limpin.

Heidi was born in Texas, and attempted to reside in as many cities in that state as possible. She made it to Houston, Lubbock, Austin, and El Paso. After spending a decade in southern California, she now lives in Eastern Washington state with her husband, their two cats, her laptop, and her Kindle. Being from the South, she often contemplates the magic of snow.

You can find Heidi on her blog.

www.ingramcontent.com/pod-product-compliance
Lightning Source LLC
Chambersburg PA
CBHW021039130626
46552CB00005B/1914

* 9 7 8 0 9 8 8 2 0 6 8 5 4 *